The Memory Quilt

A Tale of
Friends & Family
Lost & Found
in the Great
Cloquet Fire
of 1918

D1563782

Pamela J. Erickson

et al.

Cover photograph by Janelle Peterson
Cover model: Malinda Morawetz

ISBN 1-931945-08-X

Library of Congress Catalog Number: 2003112782

Printed in the United States of America

First Printing: December 2003

07 06 05 04 03   5 4 3 2 1

et al. Publishing
An imprint of Expert Publishing, Inc.
14314 Thrush Street NW,
Andover, MN 55304-3330
1-877-755-4966
www.ExpertPublishingInc.com

Andover,
Minnesota

For my nieces, Malinda, Jade, and Grace

Pamela J. Erickson

*L*isa Hanson had the flu. Every muscle, every joint ached. The light pierced her eyes, and her head felt like it was going to explode.

"Even my hair hurts."

"I know, honey. Take this, it should help." Her mother put two Advil tablets and a glass of water on her bedside table.

"Where did I get this? Nobody I know at school has it."

"I thought you said the new boy in your Spanish class was out with the flu." Louise Hanson draped a second baby blue sheet blanket on top of her daughter.

"Yeah, but I don't sit by him. I don't even remember his name."

"Shirley says the flu season started unusually early this year, and they've already seen two cases at the clinic. She says flu shots won't be available until next week."

"Did Aunt Shirley say how long this lasts?" Lisa crossed her fingers under the blankets. *Please, let it be just a couple of days at the most.*

"She said it could be as long as a week to ten days. Which reminds me, I'd better call the Martins," her mother continued. "There's no way you're going to be able to baby-sit for them tomorrow. I hope she can find someone else on such short notice. Do you think Beth would be able to do it?"

Lisa opened one eye and looked at her mother. She'd completely forgotten she was supposed to baby-sit for the neighbors next door on Saturday. The Martins were going to a wedding and would be gone most of the afternoon and into the evening; she could have made a mint! Now her best friend Beth would get the job and the money.

"Okay," her mother said, "I'll take that as a yes, and give Beth a call. You know, your dad and I are supposed to meet Shirley and Don for an early dinner tonight, then we were going to see a movie. I think I should call and cancel. You shouldn't be alone when you're this sick."

"Thanks, but I'm just going to sleep." Lisa gave her mother a weak smile and pulled the covers a little higher. "You guys go to the movie. I'll be fine."

"Are you sure?"

"I'm sure."

"Okay. But just in case, I'm taking my cell phone. If you need anything, call. And take the Advil, you'll feel better. I'll come and check on you before I leave." Her mother smiled back and closed the bedroom door softly behind her.

Her mom was trying, but it just wasn't the same. Lisa couldn't remember the last time she'd been this sick, but knew her grandma would have found a way to make her feel better.

When Lisa was growing up, her mom had always worked full-time—she taught third grade—so when Lisa or her sisters got sick and had to stay home from school, Grandma Inga, their dad's mom, would come over and take care of them.

Grandma Inga would bring her special homemade chicken soup with dumplings, a stack of Little Golden Books and her varnished wooden box lined with faded red velvet that held an old stereoscope. She and Lisa would spend the day reading the books and making up their own stories using the three-dimensional photo cards of European castles, cities of the world, and men, women, and children in various poses as story cues and illustrations.

While the stories and characters were always different, the general theme was the same—fate was at the heart of everything that happened or didn't happen, the people you met or didn't meet, the places you went, the things you saw.

"Everything happens for a reason," her grandma always said. "You may not understand it at the time, but there are bigger forces at work."

Though she missed her grandma all the time, right now Lisa missed her more than ever. She knew she was feeling sorry for herself, but Lisa couldn't help it, and wished her grandma was still here to take care of her and nurse her through the flu, like Grandma Inga used to do when Lisa was a little girl.

There was a knock on Lisa's bedroom door, and her mother came in the room carrying a big, thick quilt. "This is the first time you've really been sick since your grandma died, and I know how much you miss her. Since she can't be here, I thought I'd bring you the next best thing."

Grandma Inga had called it her "memory quilt." She'd made it herself, cutting and hand-stitching together the colorful solid and printed pieces of fabric that formed the "crazy quilt" pattern over the first two winters of her marriage, down-time on the farm before she and Grandpa John started their family.

Lisa always loved that quilt. As a small child, she traced the odd shapes and different pieces of fabric with her fingers, making up her own stories of where each piece came from—the sapphire-blue fabric was from the dress of a princess, the cream-colored material came from the shirt of the peasant who loved her, and the crimson piece from the vest of the king, who would only allow his daughter to marry a prince.

Lisa had been thrilled to receive the quilt as a gift from her grandma on her tenth birthday, and it always covered her bed until her grandma died last year. Then it became a painful reminder, and Lisa put the quilt in the back of the linen closet so she wouldn't have to look at it every night.

"Thanks, Mom," Lisa said, taking the quilt from her mother and hugging it to her chest. "I was feeling a little cold."

"I'm leaving now. I made you a turkey sandwich in case you get hungry. It's in the refrigerator. The movie gets done around 9:00, so we should be back by 9:15 or so. You sure you're going to be okay? I'll stay if you want me to."

"Mom, I'm fourteen, not four," she said. "I'll be fine. I'll call you if I need you."

"Okay. See you in a couple of hours. Get some rest now."

A flood of warm wonderful memories washed over Lisa as she spread the quilt out across her bed. She thought of how when she was younger, her grandma would brush her hair before bed and they'd laugh as they watched the sparks crackle in the dark, of how her grandma would tell Lisa stories about growing up on a farm with her three sisters and two brothers (and no electricity or indoor plumbing), and, most memorable of all, of her account of the great fire of 1918 that burned the towns of Cloquet and Moose Lake, Minnesota, to the ground.

Everyone in her grandma's family, except the oldest daughter, Liisa, survived the fire by laying in the bottom of a gravel pit dug to build the foundation of a new barn and covering themselves with wet rugs and blankets. In fact, Lisa's grandma used the blanket that saved her that day as the batting for the inside of her quilt. She'd never said so, but Lisa had always suspected that was why her grandma called it her "memory quilt."

Though her parents had chosen to use the American spelling rather than the Finnish spelling, Lisa had been named for her grandma's oldest sister. Liisa had been in town the day of the fire, not in the gravel pit with the rest of her family on the farm. She was known to have gotten on one of the trains carrying people out of Cloquet to safety, but had never been seen again. No one knew what happened to her—a family mystery that Lisa hadn't thought about for quite a while.

Shivering, Lisa tucked the quilt around her. It made her feel like her grandma was still here, watching over her, taking care of her. As she drifted off to sleep, Lisa thought she could hear her grandma's voice saying her name and asking, as she did when Lisa was a child, if a story would make her feel better.

Chapter

"Liisa. Liisa."

Someone was calling her name. Her head didn't hurt anymore, but something was tickling her nose. Lisa slowly opened her eyes—and saw sky.

She was outside, lying on her back in a field of tall, dancing grass, the sun shining warmly on her upturned face. Lisa put her hands on the ground, sat up, and looked around. Where was she and how did she get here? A young girl wearing a mid-length dress the color of butter beneath a much-patched cream-colored pinafore was walking towards her, apparently coming from the small log house she could see in the distance.

As she was about to wipe her hands off on her clothes, Lisa looked down to see that she was wearing a gray-blue dress and an off-white apron that nearly covered the front of her dress from neck to hem. Around her neck hung a royal blue scarf with tiny white flowers, and her shoes were like boots that came up just above her ankles and laced-up like ice skates. "Toto," she said to herself, aloud, "we're not in Kansas anymore."

"Liisa, what are you doing here? You told Mother you'd go find Millie. Did you find her? Pedar's here and he's ready to go back to town. He's waiting for you."

Lisa stared at the girl in disbelief. She knew that face; it had stared back at her a hundred times from an old photo in the family album. It was her Grandma Inga, looking just a little older than she did in the photo taken of her family about ten months, her grandma had told her, before the Cloquet fire. It was the only photo Lisa's dad had of his mother's parents; his grandfather had died two months after the photo was taken. It was also the last known photo of Inga's then 14-year-old sister, Liisa.

At this age, the "Lisa" Inga knew was her sister, not her granddaughter. Is that who her grandma thought she was?

"Oh, there she is. Ever since that cow figured out how to open the gate, she always gets into Mr. Koski's field. Is that where you found her? For some reason, she likes his grass better than ours," Inga said, plopping into Lisa's lap and putting her arms around her older sister's neck. "I wish you didn't have to go back to the McClains' already. I really miss you, Liisa. When you're gone, I don't have anyone to talk to. Hannah and Ida tease me all the time and call me a baby. I'm not a baby. I'm eight years old. Arvo's the baby, he's only five."

"I miss you too," Lisa said, smiling at the childish pout on Inga's face. "You have no idea how much," she added, as she hugged this younger version of her grandma.

A small whirlwind of dirt and leaves gusted around them, and Lisa lovingly pushed back the hair that had blown across Inga's face. Such a simple act, but Lisa had been on the receiving end of her grandma doing the same thing to her so many times. The role reversal made her smile, yet she felt tears begin to sting her eyes.

"Don't you have something to tie your hair back? This wind is really getting strong."

"I must have lost my scarf somewhere. I remember having it on when we went in for dinner, but I don't know where it is now," Inga said, pushing her long blonde hair out of her face again.

"Here, take mine." Lisa removed the scarf from around her neck and tied it under Inga's chin. "This should keep your hair out of your face. My hair's pinned up and won't blow around like yours."

Lisa almost laughed out loud as her hands inadvertently reached up to touch the bun on top of her head. A bun? Lisa wore her hair pulled back in a ponytail when she played basketball, but she'd never in her whole life worn her hair in a bun. Only old ladies and ballerinas wore buns.

This had to be a dream! She was sick and had fallen asleep thinking about her grandma, and now she was dreaming about her grandma's oldest sister, Liisa. Actually, that she was Liisa.

And yet, it all seemed so real, the wind, the grass, her grandma.

"Isn't this the scarf Mrs. McClain gave you? It's your favorite. What if I lose it?"

"You need it more than I do right now. Take it."

Inga gave Lisa a hug and stood up. "Thanks. Should I tell Pedar you're coming?"

"Yes. And the next time Hannah and Ida pick on you, tell them I said they should leave you alone, or they'll have to answer to me." Lisa knew all too well what it was like having older sisters tease you just because you were the youngest. Being the oldest could be kind of fun.

As she watched Inga turn and run back towards the house, Lisa smiled. It was strange to think of her grandma as a young girl. She'd seen the old photo so many times, and knew some of the stories about her life growing up, but never really thought about what her grandma must have been like as a person.

It also made her think about Liisa, and how hard it must have been for her grandma, then only eight years old, to lose her home and her sister all in the same day. Ever since she found out that she'd been named for her grandma's oldest sister, Lisa had been more than curious about what could have happened to her. Was that why she was dreaming about her?

Lisa stood up and half-walked, half-ran down the small hill towards a wagon led by a team of horses, one white, one gray, standing between the small log house and what appeared to be an old hen house, its red paint faded and peeling.

"I've got the eggs and the butter your mother made yesterday for the store," said the young man sitting in the front of the wagon. "And, she gave you some of her special biscuits to bring to Mrs. McClain. Urho helped me load everything. He just left for town to get new shoes for the horse. If we hurry, we can catch up to him."

"And break the eggs? No, Pedar, you drive slowly," said a woman stepping into the open doorway from inside the house. "If you break the eggs, we have to give Mr. Murphy and the Companies Store back their money, and we need the money."

Though Lisa barely recognized her, she knew it was her great-grandmother, Helen Maki, from the old family photo. She looked older in person than she did in the photo, a lot older.

Lisa tried to picture Helen as a young bride arriving in Cloquet from Oulu, Finland. Grandma Inga told Lisa many times how Inga's father, William, came to Minnesota first, and his wife followed six months later.

"My father went to meet my mother at the train when she came in," her grandma told Lisa. "He was wearing a straw hat, riding a bicycle, and chewing gum. And my mother thought, 'Oh my God, is that how much America's changed him?' She said she would have gone back to Finland right then and there if she had the money, but she didn't."

Today Helen looked so tired, so life-weary. Her hair had turned the same soft faded gray as the weather-washed logs of the house, and her skirt mirrored the dry, brown grass that carpeted the front yard. On the step below her sat a young boy holding a wriggling orange tabby kitten, its high-pitched mews and luminescent green eyes contrasted sharply with the sad gray eyes and quiet, joyless expression on the boy's face.

"We need the money," Helen repeated, looking at Lisa, attempting to hide the desperation in her voice with a forced smile. "Without the money you make working for the McClains, I don't know how we'd feed your brothers. Urho and Arvo eat twice as much as the girls. And Arvo's outgrown his shoes again."

Helen looked down at her youngest son, and Lisa couldn't help but smile. Her grandma's brother, Arvo, had grown to be well over six feet, quite tall for a man of his time. Yet today, he appeared to be drowning in the shirt and pants he wore. Hand-me-downs from his older brother, Urho, Lisa decided.

"Pedar, thank you for letting Liisa ride with you when you make your deliveries. I'd never get to see her otherwise. And Liisa, don't forget to tell Mrs. McClain my thoughts and prayers are with Matt. She must be so worried about him. I'm just glad Urho is too young to be drafted—but don't tell her I said that," she said, obviously embarrassed by her last statement.

"Liisa, we've got to go. Mr. Murphy will want to close the store by 7:00, and I need to get your mother's eggs and butter in the store root cellar and write up all my delivery sheets before then," Pedar said, motioning for her to get in the wagon.

Lisa turned to look at Helen, then back at Pedar. Her eyes scanned the yard as she tried to think of what she should do. Common sense told her she shouldn't go off with a total stranger. And yet, it was obvious they all expected her to go with Pedar—as if she had any control over where this dream was going to take her.

"If you're looking for your sisters, I asked Hannah and Ida to rake leaves and clear some of the brush between the sauna and the barn. I'm worried about all these fires we've had this fall. I'll tell them you said goodbye. Now get going. You should have left half an hour ago," Helen said. "The wind is really picking up, and I don't like the look of that sky. It's such a strange color. There must be another fire burning somewhere, because I can smell smoke."

Pedar stretched out his hand to help her up on the wagon seat. As she looked into his face for the first time, Lisa felt an unexpected flutter that started in her chest and flipped-flopped its way up to her throat. At first glance, he was average looking and his straight blond hair was cut much shorter than any of the guys Lisa knew at school. But boy did his eyes twinkle! A person could easily drown in those optical pools, she thought. They were so blue, almost cornflower blue, and his smile—well that was another story. On second glance, even with that dorky haircut, he was cute—very cute.

The flush she felt rise to her face was so real, so hot, that Lisa wondered for a moment whether this was really a dream. But it had to be, didn't it? Why was she dreaming about a young man who made her insides do back-flips like an Olympic gymnast? Lisa stole a sideways glance at Pedar as he urged the horses forward, her eyes gravitating to his strong, muscular forearms as they worked the reins.

Just as she was starting to imagine what it might be like to slowdance in those arms, her head resting on his broad shoulders, her daydream was interrupted by two blonde bookends, one in a red dress, the other in a blue dress, who ran out from behind the barn and towards the wagon, waving. "Bye, Liisa," they yelled in unison.

"Goodbye, Mother. Goodbye, Inga. Arvo. Hannah. Ida. Goodbye." Lisa waved to all of them as the wagon started to move. Everything in this dream was happening so fast. She felt torn between wanting to stay and spend more time with these people (they were her family), and wanting to know more about Liisa. And, she had to admit to herself, getting to know more about Pedar. Plus, if she didn't go, sooner or later she'd say or do something wrong, and they'd realize she wasn't really Liisa.

Grandma Inga never really talked about how hard it had been for her mother, or the rest of her family, after her father's death. She was only seven years old when he died, and probably too young to understand what her father's death meant to the family. It had been the fire and the disappearance of her sister that haunted her throughout her entire adult life. At least with Inga's father, there had been a funeral and closure. With her sister, Liisa, there were only questions.

The sky *was* a strange color, Lisa thought as she looked up. Wisps of cotton candy seemed to float in a sea of thick gray haze. As they drove through fall's palette of brilliant red, yellow, and orange hues, the realization hit with the impact of a pop fly dropping into her catcher's mitt. It was so obvious! Why had it taken her so long to see it?

"Pedar, what day is it?"

"It's Saturday, of course."

"No, I mean what month, what day?"

"October 12th," Pedar said, looking at her as though she'd lost her mind.

"1918?"

"No, 1920. Of course it's 1918. Are you okay?"

October 12, 1918. The day the city of Cloquet burned to the ground.

*L*isa nervously scanned the tree-lined horizon from her seat on the wagon, twisting around until she saw smoke behind them on her right—it still appeared to be quite far away. She didn't have a clue where she was or how long it would take to get into town. None of the local landmarks she was familiar with were visible, and she'd never known exactly where her grandma's family farm was before the fire, only that it was northeast of town, presumably off what Lisa knew as the North Road. After the fire, the Maki family started over and bought property west of town. She'd been to that farmhouse. Her grandma's brother, Arvo, lived there with his wife, Mayme, and raised dairy cows until he died a couple of years ago.

"What are you looking at?" Pedar asked, interrupting her thoughts.

"Do you see the smoke back there on the right? How far away do you think it is?"

"I'd say at least ten, fifteen miles," Pedar said, looking over his right shoulder. "Don't worry." He put his hand on her arm. "It's probably just a farmer clearing land. Or another brush fire. It'll burn itself out, like the others."

The warmth of his hand on her arm felt like fire itself, and Lisa's face flushed hot again. Pedar smiled reassuringly and pulled his hand back to the reins.

Lisa tried to concentrate on what she could remember about the fire. While much of what she knew came from her grandma's stories, she'd also learned a lot about it from her Minnesota history class in sixth grade.

The Cloquet fire started with a spark from a passing train near the small town of Brookston, approximately fifteen miles northwest of Cloquet. The fall of 1918 had been exceptionally dry, and many small fires started in the area but died out on their own. While people were watchful, they had also grown accustomed to the fires that sprung up every fall, so the first signs of smoke didn't originally cause much alarm. In fact, many people were caught by surprise, forced to flee on a moment's notice.

Cloquet's principle industry—then and now—revolved around trees and lumber, and the vast majority of the town's buildings, and even some of the sidewalks, were made of wood. Only the new brick Garfield school, a few buildings on Dunlap Island in the middle of the St. Louis River, and three of the town's five busy sawmills survived the fire. Everything else disappeared in the flames.

"Liisa, are you okay? You're pretty quiet, and that's not like you," Pedar teased.

If you only knew, Lisa thought. "I'm fine," she said. "I was just thinking about how sad she seems—Mother, I mean. I wish there was more I could do to help her out."

"You heard what she said; she couldn't make it without the money you make working for the McClains. You're doing as much as you can. Speaking of money, did I tell you

Mr. McClain is going to let me drive one of the company tote teams this winter? With so many men gone fighting the Germans, he's giving some of us younger guys a chance to deliver supplies to the lumber camps. I'll be making more money, a lot more money. Mrs. Tillman's boarding house is fine for now, but I really want my own place."

"Your own house? Really?" He seemed awfully young to want the responsibility of owning a home.

"I turn eighteen next week," he said as if he'd read her thoughts. "I'm hoping the war will be over before they have another draft, and I get called. Your mother said Urho was too young to be drafted. How old is he?"

Lisa had to think. She knew Liisa was fourteen at the time of the fire, and Urho was two years older, so he would be . . .

"Sixteen," said Lisa. "Urho's only sixteen."

"Your father used to work the boom house for Mr. McClain during the winter. Is Urho going to try and get a job with the lumber camp? He's pretty young, but I know the Weyerhaeuser mills are short of men and would probably be willing to hire him. 'Specially if you talked to Mr. McClain."

If history stayed on course, it wouldn't matter whether she talked to Mr. McClain or not. Though three of the town's sawmills would survive, the supply of white pine had already started to disappear. And what was left in the area would burn in the fire. It would be months before the mills became fully productive again, and Urho would be busy finding their family—and what few cows they had left—a new place to live.

"Mrs. McClain must really be worried about Matt. With all her work for the Red Cross, she knows how many soldiers are dying in the training camps from the flu," Pedar said, turning to look at Lisa, who remained quiet. She didn't have a clue what he was talking about.

He continued, "Carl Swedberg was at Camp Grant with Matt. He got the flu and died in a week. I heard his body's coming back today on the train. His funeral's supposed to be tomorrow."

An uncomfortable silence hung thick between them, and Lisa felt she needed to say something, but what?

"I'm sorry," Pedar said, seeing the shocked look on Lisa's face. "I didn't know you and Matt were so close."

War? Soldiers dying from the flu? They hadn't been in her grandma's stories about the fire. She knew almost nothing about either, so how could she be dreaming about them? Lisa made a mental note to look both of them up on the Internet when she woke up—assuming, that is, that she was dreaming all of this.

"I'll drop you off at the McClains' first and then go over to the store."

"I'm sorry, what did you say?"

"Didn't you tell me you had to be back by 5:00 so you could help Mrs. McClain get ready for her Red Cross meeting? Her class on rolling bandages? We're running a little late so I'll drop you off at the McClains' and then go over to the store to drop off the eggs and butter."

Lisa had been so lost in her own thoughts that she'd completely forgotten that her grandma's sister had been a domestic for one of the wealthiest families in Cloquet. She had no idea what that meant. Sure, Lisa could cook, but that usually meant a frozen pizza or microwave popcorn. She hadn't done any actual cooking from scratch since she'd worked on her Girl Scout Cooking Badge nearly five years earlier. Plus, this was 1918. What kind of stove did the McClains have? Had vacuum cleaners been invented yet? How did people do laundry? Did they have running water? Lisa's head was spinning. How would she ever pass as a maid?

What frightened her even more was that she was beginning to believe she really was here—that this wasn't a dream. She really *was* back in the past, about to experience the worst day of her grandma's life, and maybe Liisa's too.

4
Chapter

It wasn't until the wagon started down the hill of what Lisa knew as Highway 33 that she finally got her bearings. She could see the root beer-colored water of the St. Louis River below and the silver water tower on the hill in Pinehurst Park. Ahead, a bridge crossed over to Dunlap Island's north shore, with a second bridge off the south shore leading into Cloquet's west end business district.

Lisa always loved this bird's eye view of Cloquet. The familiar surroundings made her feel a little less panicked. On the other hand, the smell of smoke grew stronger and the wind blew so hard, it could easily turn a decent umbrella inside out. Overhead, the sun glowed like a red ball of fire through the growing haze of smoke.

The loud, staccato whistle of a train pierced the air just as Lisa and Pedar crossed the first bridge onto Dunlap Island. A train was pulling into the Union Depot, its whistle screaming every thirty seconds.

"Why is he blowing the whistle like that?" Pedar asked, more to himself, Lisa thought, than to her.

As they began to cross the second bridge into Cloquet, they could see people hanging out the windows of the passenger train, waving their arms wildly. Pedar reined the horses in and pulled the wagon to the side of the depot's platform, wanting to see what was going on. A montage of voices cried out from the incoming train.

"Brookston's on fire!"

"The whole town's gone!"

"It's coming this way!"

Drawn by the anxious-sounding whistle, the small crowd gathered at the depot spread out down the platform to talk to the agitated Brookston refugees as the train came to a stop. The black paint on the cars was burned and blistered. The passengers looked no better, covered with soot, weary, yet animated, from their ordeal.

"Are you getting off here?" a man wearing a Union Depot uniform asked the engineer.

"No. The fire's headed this way. We're going on to Superior. But we could use some water and bandages. It's taken us over an hour to get here from Brookston because of the fire and smoke on the tracks, and some of these people have been injured."

The man in the uniform looked over at Pedar and the wagon. "Pedar, drive over to the Northeastern and see what you can get for these people. And you, Charlie Berg," he said to a boy about eight with a bicycle, "go get Doc Sinclair. There's people here that need his help."

"Sure thing, Mr. Fauley," Pedar said, tapping the horses with the reins. "We'll get whatever we can."

Fauley called to a tall man standing on the platform, "Tom, go in the depot and call Chief McSweeney and the mayor. They need to know about this." Then he climbed aboard the train to talk to the engineer.

As the tall man ran into the depot, the boy with the bicycle sped off down Vine Street, turning the corner at Avenue C, obviously taking his mission very seriously.

So that was who Fauley Park was named after, Lisa thought, her left hand holding tightly to the back of the wagon seat and her right hand holding even tighter to the seat's edge as Pedar turned the wagon back towards Dunlap Island. She didn't know what to do. Would history be changed because she was here, or had she been part of history when it was made the first time? She had to assume she was here for a reason. Lisa decided to follow her instincts.

"You stay here," Pedar said to Lisa as they pulled up behind the building Lisa recognized as the Northeastern Hotel. "I'll see what I can get from the hotel."

"Let me help you carry some things," Lisa said, turning to jump down from the wagon.

"No!" Pedar said. "I shouldn't have even brought you back here with me. Nice girls do not go in the Northeastern! Your mother and Mrs. McClain would have my head."

"But this is an emergency. I'm sure they'd understand."

"No!" Pedar said again. "I don't have time to argue with you. I'll go and get whatever I can from the hotel, and you can help me load up the wagon. Don't move. I'll be right back."

She appreciated his concern for Liisa Maki's honor and reputation—at least it showed he cared about her—but saying she couldn't go in the hotel just because she was a girl was ridiculous! But then, she remembered, women wouldn't even have the right to vote for a few more years.

To her surprise, the Northeastern was actually a nice looking building in 1918. Eighty-some years later, it looked as though it'd been through a war—its orange-brown bricks cracked and crumbling, the walls pock-marked with holes where some of the bricks had fallen out. The whole island looked so different; all of the bars in town were confined right here, along Main Street and St. Louis Avenue. She had never imagined Dunlap Island could be this busy. In her time, Spafford Park—a hangout for RV and canoe enthusiasts—took up most of the island, and only two bars and the Northeastern Hotel still conducted business.

About five minutes after he'd gone in, Pedar came out of the hotel with an armload of white bed sheets. "Here's your chance to use what you've learned from Mrs. McClain," he said handing them off to Lisa. "We'll have to do our own bandage rolling. Start ripping. The manager says he doesn't have any bandages. I'm going back for another load."

Lisa took the pile of bed sheets and placed them next to her on the wagon seat, not really sure what she was supposed to do next.

"Check the metal box in the back of the wagon. I keep a few tools with me just in case something happens to the wagon or the harnesses when I'm out delivering in the country. There should be a knife in there," Pedar said over his shoulder as he went back into the hotel.

Lisa climbed over the back of the seat and into the wagon bed. She opened a black painted metal box and found the knife, which she brought back with her to the seat, and picked up one of the sheets. Pushing the knife through the sheet about an inch from the edge, she slid it through the selvage and began to tear, mimicking what she'd seen women do in the movies and on TV. By the time Pedar came out of the hotel again, she'd finished one sheet, rolling the strips into small, jellyroll-like balls that she placed in the wooden box that also held the eggs in the back of the wagon.

"How's it going?" Pedar asked, putting an armload of towels and blankets on the seat next to her.

"Fine. But I'm never going to get all of these done in time. The train's got to be leaving soon."

"Do as many as you can. We'll just give them to who-ever's in charge, and they can roll their own bandages on the way. Besides, they might actually need the sheets just as they are once they get to Superior. Mr. Murphy's daughter, Bridgit, called from Duluth this morning and told him both Duluth and Superior closed down yesterday because of the influenza epidemic. I don't know where these people are going to go once they get there."

"Closed down?" Closing schools and businesses because of blizzards or freezing temperatures wasn't an everyday occurrence, even in Minnesota, though it usually happened once during the winter months, maybe twice. But Lisa had never heard of a town closing because of flu.

"Well, not closed down exactly. Bridget said the city commissioners closed all the public buildings, like schools, churches, and restaurants. They think if they can keep crowds of people from getting together, they can stop the flu from spreading. These people should just stay here. There must be, what, 200 people on that train? Between houses and hotels, we can put them up."

"Pedar, you heard what they said. The fire's coming this way. Cloquet's going to burn, too. The whole town will be gone by tomorrow morning."

"No." Pedar shook his head in disagreement. "The fire department will build a fire break outside of town. They've done it before. It won't reach us."

She admired his willingness to get involved, and was impressed with his calm under pressure. But he, along with everyone else, thought this was just another fire. Lisa knew that if she did nothing else while she was here, she had to make them realize this wasn't business as usual. This fire was different. This one they wouldn't be able to control.

5
Chapter

"*L*iisa. What are you doing here?"

I wish I knew, Lisa thought. Not only what she was doing here, but how she got here. She turned to see who had called her name and saw a blond young man in faded overalls driving an old weather-beaten wagon pulled by one large brown horse coming towards her.

"She's helping me, Urho. We're getting supplies for the people from Brookston," Pedar said, coming out from around the back of his wagon. "Don't worry, I didn't let her go in the Northeastern."

"I don't care about that." Urho turned to look back at Lisa. "I thought you had to be back at the McClains' by 5:00. It's way past that now. Do you want to lose your job? Liisa, do you think anyone else in this town would hire you if you were fired by the McClains?"

So this was Urho, Liisa's older brother. He died long before Lisa was born, so she'd never met him as an adult, and if this was any indication of what he was like, she was kind of glad.

Lisa felt confused—and hurt—at his accusatory tone. Would she get Liisa in trouble? She could only assume that if Mrs. McClain was as involved in the Red Cross as Pedar implied, she would expect Liisa and Pedar to do everything they could. "I won't get fired," Lisa said with as much confidence as she could muster. "Mrs. McClain would want me to help these people. What are you doing here? I thought you came to town to get new shoes for the horse. You can't be done already."

"I heard about Brookston when I was at the livery. I decided to get the horse shod another time and go back home. If the fire heads our way, I have to be there. Mother and the girls can't save the farm by themselves."

"You won't be able to stop it, if it does reach the farm," Lisa replied. "This fire's too big."

Urho must have thought she was criticizing him, instead of warning him. "You might be making most of the money, but I'm responsible for the farm and the family since Father died. You think I want to be in charge? I'm only sixteen..."

"Sorry to break up this lovely family gathering," Pedar interrupted, "but we've got to get this stuff to the train before it leaves." He pulled himself up on the wagon and sat down in the seat, grabbing the reins.

"Don't worry, I'll get Liisa back to the McClains' right after we drop this off. And I'll explain everything to Mrs. McClain. She likes me." Pedar grinned at Urho. "I'll make sure Liisa doesn't get in trouble."

"Yeah, right." Urho looked at both of them with disdain. "I've got to go," he said, urging his horse forward with a tap of his reins.

"Urho, think about the family first and the farm second," Lisa called after him. "If the fire gets to the farm, take everybody down to the gravel pit we dug for the barn's foundation. Cover yourselves with wet blankets or rugs and wait it out. Don't try and save the buildings. With this wind, you won't have a chance."

It had worked before, and Lisa felt it couldn't hurt giving him the idea, though she wasn't even sure Urho had heard her. He never looked back. She hated to think that the last words he and Liisa had said to each other were angry ones.

Pedar turned the wagon around and headed back over the river, towards the depot.

"Pedar, over here," Mr. Fauley called, waving him over to the west end of the depot platform. "We'll unload everything up here, and the volunteers can pass things out down the train. The engineer wants to get going. I've called ahead, and the Superior Red Cross is opening up the armory for these people."

"Want to wait for me, or do you want to run home from here?" Pedar asked Lisa.

"I'll wait. I may need you to help me explain to Mrs. McClain why I'm so late. Remember, she likes you." Lisa had no idea where the McClains lived, though she assumed it was on Park Place. That had been the wealthier area of town before the fire, and still claimed some of the bigger, older homes in Cloquet, many of them some of the first homes rebuilt after the fire.

Pedar smiled as he jumped down to the ground. "Okay, stay here. I shouldn't be too long."

The depot was buzzing with activity. Women wearing Red Cross uniforms and others with just sashes over their regular clothes were helping a small group of men unload food, clothing, and medical supplies from three other wagons. A baby was crying. Some of the people on the train appeared to be in shock, as they stared numbly with blank eyes at the volunteers trying to offer them food and water. One woman, her face streaked with soot and tears, walked up to each train car, asking between sobs if anyone had seen her children.

"Liisa! There you are. I was so worried!"

Lisa turned to see a woman in full Red Cross uniform walking hurriedly towards her.

"Mrs. McClain," she heard Pedar say from behind her. "I'm sorry I didn't get Liisa home by 5:00, but we stopped to help. I'll get her home as soon as we're done unloading the supplies we picked up at the Northeastern—I picked up at the Northeastern. Liisa waited in the wagon."

"I'm just glad to know you're both okay. I was afraid you might have gotten trapped by the fire. Go, help. I've got work to do myself," Mrs. McClain said, using the Red Cross manual in her hand to point at the train. "Mr. Fauley called me about Brookston and I had to leave before you got back, so I left you a note on the dining room table. Once you've finished here, could you go get Mary and bring her home? She's over visiting at a friend's, Sara Watson, on Third Street. She won't want to come home—I'd told her she could stay for supper and go to the movie—but tell her I told you to come and get her. God forbid that something should happen, but I don't want to end up like that poor woman, looking all over for my children. I want to know where Mary is, and that she's safe. I want her home."

Lisa saw Pedar hesitate, and realized he was trying to figure out how much trouble he'd be in if he picked up Mary before he brought the wagonload of eggs and butter to the store.

"Don't worry, Mrs. McClain. As soon as we're done here, we'll get Mary and bring her home," Pedar said.

"Thank you. I've got to coordinate a relief effort with the Duluth and Superior Red Cross, so I'm not sure how long I'll be here. Tell Mary I said she's to stay home. I don't want her going anywhere tonight. I tried calling Mr. McClain at the mill, but he wasn't in his office. If he calls, tell him where I am. I don't know where Michael is, but if he calls or comes home, tell him I want him to come home, and stay home, too.

"And Liisa, no point in making a big supper—I doubt that Mr. McClain or I will be there. So just make something for Mary and Michael. Thanks again," Mrs. McClain called over her shoulder, as if she were simply giving a babysitter instructions before an evening out.

Cook something? How could she be thinking of food at a time like this? Of course, Lisa reasoned, Mrs. McClain didn't know what was going to happen, but Lisa did. As far as cooking supper for the McClain children—well, she'd like to avoid that potential fiasco for as long as possible.

"Why don't you climb into the wagon and hand everything to me. I think we'll get done a lot faster if you help," Pedar said, breaking into her impending panic attack.

"Sure. No problem."

In less than ten minutes, Pedar was back on the wagon seat driving the two of them up Vine Street. For Lisa, the drive was excitingly surreal. This was Cloquet, and yet it wasn't—at least it wasn't the Cloquet she knew. The streets were laid out in the same patterns, but everything looked so different.

In 1918, the business district seemed to be concentrated in the west end of town—the White Front Café, the O'Donnell House hotel, O. J. Fryklund & Son Jewelers, Proulx's Drugstore, Fish Hardware. Lisa couldn't help but stare at the strange names on the unfamiliar buildings as she and Pedar drove past. In Lisa's Cloquet, the business district was in the east end along Cloquet Avenue, with a second retail Mecca rapidly growing along the Highway 33 corridor, following the lead of a Wal-Mart that had simultaneously opened its doors and killed off several local businesses.

Lisa could see the back of the Presbyterian Church and the steeple of the Catholic Church up on the hill to the left. The library sat on Cloquet Avenue where the Carlton County Historical Society stood in her time. It had been the local library until the town built a new one off Fourteenth Street. Across the street, where the bank was today, stood the mill horse barns, filled with horses. Ordinarily the horses would pull the tote wagons and the loads of cut logs in just a couple of weeks. Hard to believe that all of these beautiful wooden buildings would disappear, but the saloons and the Northeastern Hotel on Dunlap Island would survive.

What amazed Lisa most were the boards of wood stacked in piles at least six feet high lining Cloquet Avenue on the river side, continuing east as far as Eighth Street. It was when Pedar mentioned (in a voice that told her she should already know this), that there were more stacks, bigger stacks along the river to the west of the depot, in the lumberyard known as Bottle Alley, that Lisa realized she'd been staring at the stacks, her mouth open in astonishment. Like a fuse to dynamite, Lisa could see that the fire would follow these wooden stacks into town, the resulting explosion of fire, wood, and wind consuming Cloquet in short order.

Another surprise were the cars—not Model Ts, but they looked just as old to Lisa—a few parked here and there and some driving up and down the streets. Why, she wondered, did Pedar still drive this bouncing old wagon when he could use a truck? So, she asked him.

"The roads out in the country are so full of holes and ruts, with a truck, I'd be doing nothing but getting stuck and trying to pull myself out, or fixing flat tires," he said. "I don't have that problem with the wagon."

The intensity on Pedar's face reflected his concern about getting his load back to the store and still keeping his promise to Mrs. McClain. He was so caught up in being responsible and taking care of everyone and everything that Lisa felt the need to offer some kind of solution.

"If you need to get back to the store, you can just let me off at the Watsons' and Mary and I can walk home. It's not really that far," Lisa said, crossing her fingers. *Please say no, please say no.* She'd only known him about two hours, but she didn't know Mary at all. It would be so much easier if he came along as a buffer.

"I promised Mrs. McClain that *we'd* take Mary home. Besides, what can Mr. Murphy do to me? The Northern and Cloquet Lumber Companies own the Companies Store. Mr. McClain manages the Northern Lumber Company and Mr. Murphy manages the Companies Store. So really, Mr. McClain is one of Mr. Murphy's bosses. Mrs. McClain asked me to do her a favor, and I don't think it would be a good idea to ignore her," Pedar said, smiling at Lisa.

Whew! Lisa released an inward sigh of relief. She wondered how old Mary was, and if she and Liisa were close. Really, what was the worst that could happen? Still, for the moment, the meeting with Mary made Lisa even more nervous than the impending fire.

6 Chapter

Pedar turned the wagon off Cloquet Avenue onto Third Street. Lisa didn't remember the hill being this steep before. Would the horses be able to make the climb—assuming they were going up as far as Carlton Avenue? There were a lot of things she had taken for granted, and climbing this hill in a car was one of them. So were their car's shocks and comfortable seats. Her lower back and rear end screamed with displeasure at the lack of padding on the wagon's hard wooden seat.

"It's the white house with the blue trim, right?" Pedar asked, breaking into her thoughts.

Without thinking, Lisa answered, "I think so. It's been a while since I was here." Which was sort of true. Lisa couldn't even remember the last time she been down Third Street.

"You'd better go to the door. Mrs. Watson knows you and Mary listens to you. Whenever I talk to her, she just giggles."

Sounds like a crush to me, Lisa thought, and was surprised to find she was actually feeling a little jealous. Ridiculous, she admonished herself. You don't even know him.

To Pedar she nodded in agreement, and jumped down from the wagon and strode up the front walk of the Watson's house. The front door opened before she even had a chance to knock.

"Liisa?" A woman with dark brown hair piled in a bun atop her head stood in the open doorway, drying her hands on her apron.

"Mrs. McClain asked me to come pick up Mary."

"But we haven't even eaten yet. Mary's staying for supper, and then the girls and I were going to see Marguerite Clark in *The Seven Swans*."

"I know," Lisa admitted, "but Mrs. McClain would really like Mary at home—in case the fire that hit Brookston heads this way."

"The girls are going to be so disappointed. At least let Mary stay for supper. Roger will bring her home right after dessert. I promise," Mrs. Watson said.

"It's not up to me," Lisa said. "I'm just doing what Mrs. McClain asked me to."

Mrs. Watson shook her head in disbelief and shrugged her shoulders. "Okay, but I think Mrs. McClain's worried about nothing. Come in. The girls are upstairs in Sara and Coral's room. I'll go get them."

Squeals of surprise and disappointment preceded the two girls who came running down the stairs, followed by Mrs. Watson, who gave Lisa an "I told you so" look. Both looked ten or eleven and wore nearly identical navy and white sailor dresses. Obviously best friends, Lisa thought, but which one was Mary? Incredibly, before Mary even spoke, Lisa knew the answer.

"Mary, get your things. Your mother wants you to go home," she said to the girl on the right.

"Liisa, please let me stay. We're rehearsing our parts for the school play," Mary said, her lower lip protruding like a small shelf.

"I'm sorry, Mary, but your mother told Pedar and me to pick you up and bring you home. She's helping Mr. Fauley coordinate things with the Red Cross for the Brookston fire victims."

"Pedar?" Mary looked at her friend, Sara, and blushed.

Gee, Lisa smiled to herself, I'm glad to see I'm not the only one he has that effect on. "Pedar's waiting out in the wagon," she told Mary. "We've really got to get going. Thanks, Mrs. Watson, Sara."

"Yeah, thanks!" Mary said nodding to the Watsons as she pushed open the front door. Lisa watched in amazement as Mary literally skipped down the front walk to the wagon. For someone who hadn't wanted to leave just a minute ago, she seemed pretty eager now. In fact, a little too eager, Lisa thought, as she watched Mary pull herself up and onto the wagon seat, and slide in as close to Pedar as she could without actually forcing him off the seat. Amazing what a little infatuation will do!

Pedar appeared totally oblivious to Mary's obvious adoration. Lisa had barely sat down in the wagon, and the horses began moving. Definitely a man with a mission, thought Lisa.

"Mary, do you know where Michael is?" Pedar asked, as he turned the wagon around and headed back towards Cloquet Avenue. "Your mother wants him home, too."

"They thought this wind would be great for flying kites, so he and Jason Pulte went down to the flats by the river," Mary said, blushing again as she looked at Pedar through demurely lowered eyelashes. Lisa could see the little actress was still rehearsing her craft.

"Liisa, once I drop you off, call Pultes' and see if Michael and Jason are there. If they aren't, leave a message with Mr. Murphy, and after I've finished unloading the wagon, I'll go look for them."

"Can I go with you?" Mary asked. "I know where they are. You'll never find them without me."

"As much as I'd love to have your company," Pedar said, winking at Lisa over Mary's head, "I promised your mother I'd get you home. Besides, I'm pretty sure I know where they are."

Pedar turned the wagon right on Broadway and then left on Avenue C. The Brookston train was gone, but down Vine Street, the depot still bustled with activity. They continued on past Arch Street, heading towards Park Place and the McClain house.

Big, white two-story houses lined both sides of the street, monuments to their owners' wealth and positions. Pedar pulled the horses over and stopped the wagon in front of the third house on the north side of the cul-de-sac that formed Park Place. Lisa jumped down and helped Mary to the ground. The McClains' house was at least three times the size of her family's small Lincoln-log house, and probably worth a dozen times more.

"Thanks, Pedar. Are you sure I can't help you find Michael?" Mary asked.

"I'm sure."

Mary smiled, and began walking towards the house, turning back to look at Pedar every four or five steps.

"Okay," Lisa said. "I'm only supposed to leave a message if Michael and Jason aren't at the McClains' or the Pultes', right? No message means we found them, and you don't have to go look for them."

"Right," Pedar said. "Don't forget your mother's biscuits. I put them in the back next to the butter."

"Oh yeah, thanks." Lisa looked in the back of the wagon and saw, for the first time, something wrapped in what looked like a dishtowel over in the back left corner. Helen's biscuits. She walked around to the rear of the wagon and reached in and picked them up.

The front door slammed and Mary was inside.

"Looks like Mrs. McClain isn't your only fan in the family," Lisa teased, as Pedar started the horses moving towards the turn-around at the end of Park Place.

Pedar turned back to look at Lisa as he drove away, his eyes twinkling with laughter. "If I didn't know any better, Liisa Maki, I'd say you were jealous."

Lisa knew he meant it as a joke, but the barb—tossed as casually as a hat on a chair—hit just a little too close to home. She had bigger things to worry about, Lisa told herself as she climbed the stairs to the front porch and walked towards the front door. Like getting the McClains, Pedar, and Liisa out of town safely and away from the fire. But first and foremost, would she be able to figure out how to use a phone in 1918?

The phone was ringing as Lisa walked through the doorway and into the house. Liisa was the maid. Was she supposed to answer it?

"I'll get it," Mary said rushing over to the phone and picking up the receiver. "McClains', this is Mary."

Lisa had been expecting to find one of those wooden boxes with the crank on the side and the mouthpiece jutting out like an elephant's trunk, like she'd seen in all of the old movies. To her surprise, it was a black candlestick phone sitting on a small, round table at the base of the staircase in the front hall. She was familiar with the shape, but this phone had no dial. That told her everything was still done through the operator, which meant she'd have to ask to be connected to Jason Pulte's phone, actually Jason Pulte's father's phone. Did Liisa know Jason's father's name or could she ask Mary without raising suspicion? Hopefully, that was Michael on the phone and she wouldn't even have to call the Pultes'. How many times would she have to click the little arm that held the receiver before the operator answered anyway?

"Liisa, it's Papa, he wants to talk to you."

Lisa put the plate of biscuits down on a wooden chair next to the table holding the telephone, took the receiver from Mary, and spoke hesitantly into the mouthpiece. "Hello? Mr. McClain?"

"Liisa, Mary says Maggie's still down at the depot."

"Yes sir, she's working with Mr. Fauley and the Superior Red Cross. They're trying to find places for all the people from Brookston to stay tonight," Lisa said, hoping 'Maggie' was Mrs. McClain.

"I heard there's ash coming down in the west end. Did you see anything?"

"We just walked in the door, and we didn't see any on the ride back from the Watsons'. But I really think the fire's getting close and we should get ready to leave. We're trying to find Michael, and when we do, I'd like to take both Mary and Michael to the depot. I think Mr. Fauley has trains waiting to get everyone out of town."

"Let's not rush into anything. I don't think we're at that point, and I don't want to frighten Mary or Michael. What are you doing to find Michael?"

"Mary thinks he and Jason Pulte were going down by the river to fly kites. Once we hang up, I'm going to call the Pultes' to see if the boys are there. If they're not, I'm supposed to leave a message with Mr. Murphy down at the store, and once Pedar's finished unloading his wagon, he'll go look for them. Pedar said he thought he knew where they might be."

"Call the Pultes', and then call me back here at the mill and let me know if you found them. Call me even if you don't find them, okay? I'm going to try and get a hold of Maggie at the depot and see what's happening there."

Lisa promised Mr. McClain that she'd let him know what she found out, and placed the telephone receiver back in its arm. She stared at the phone. Well, it was now or never; if she was going to call the Pultes', she was going to have to try to figure out how to use this phone.

"Liisa, let me call Michael. Please?" Mary begged. "I want to tell him Mama says he has to come home. He'll be so mad if *I* tell him. Please?"

Lisa's choice was simple, embarrass herself or let Mary embarrass her brother. All things considered, really, no choice at all. "Okay, Mary. You can call the Pultes'. If Michael's there, tell him your mother wants him to come home—now, not later. If they're not there, see if the Pultes know where the boys are and when they'll be back. And then you can call Pedar and your father and let them know what you found out." Why not kill three birds with one stone?

Grinning with anticipation, Mary picked up the receiver, clicked the arm once, and spoke into the mouthpiece. "Joseph Pulte, please. Thank you. Hello, this is Mary McClain. Is Michael there?"

Lisa decided now was as good a time as any to look around the McClain house. She remembered hearing that too many people ended up with only the clothes on their backs, and since she had the advantage of knowing they had to leave, Lisa wanted to take a mental inventory of what was in the house and see what could be saved.

It was a big, beautiful house, filled with lots of dark wood and leaded glass. Lisa marveled at the intricate carvings on the posts and banister of the main staircase. From where she stood, she could see that the foyer narrowed into a hallway that appeared to go directly into the kitchen. On her left was the living room, or what they probably called the "parlor," which opened into the family dining room. To the right of the staircase was a doorway leading, Lisa found, into a combination library/office. The hardwood floors throughout were covered with rich oriental carpeting; even the hallway leading into the kitchen had a narrow runner protecting the wooden causeway beneath. To think that all of this would be ashes in just a few hours.

Lisa walked into the parlor to get a better look at the silver-framed photos so carefully arranged on a black and gold shawl-like tapestry with fringed edges that covered the top of a grand piano. The one that particularly caught her eye held a photo of the McClain family—father, mother, and three children—all staring solemnly at the camera. A recent photo, judging from Mary and Mrs. McClain; most likely taken before the oldest son, Matt, went to Camp Grant. Matt was very handsome, but Lisa had to laugh at Pedar's mistaking her silence earlier as a sign that Liisa had a crush on him. Maybe, she thought smiling to herself, it was Pedar who was jealous.

"Liisa," Mary said walking into the parlor, "I talked to Pedar and Papa. Pedar's going to go look for Michael and Jason. The Pultes haven't seen them. What are you doing?"

Lisa looked at the framed photograph still in her hand. "Mary, if the fire gets close to us and we have to leave, what would you take? I think your mother would want this photo. Can you think of anything else that's small and easy to carry that we should take with us? Important things, things that can't be replaced."

The frightened look on Mary's face told Lisa she'd done exactly what Mr. McClain had asked her not to do. "I'm sorry, Mary, I don't mean to scare you. If we have to leave, it will probably be on short notice. I just want to be prepared."

Mary looked at Lisa and then at the photo, and back at Lisa. "Mama's got a pearl necklace she got from her grandma. I think she'd want us to save that. And Papa's got a pocket watch that's been in his family for years. He keeps it in his top dresser drawer under his handkerchiefs."

"Good," Lisa said, putting the picture frame in the right pocket of her dress. "Anything else? How about clothes? Come on, you're going to have to help me rig up some kind of a sling so you can carry everything you need to take under your coat."

Surrounded by so many beautiful things and listening to Mary recite her list of irreplaceable objects, reminded Lisa of one more thing from her grandma's stories. Though the fire held the Maki family captive on their farm, a family friend, another farm girl that worked in town as a domestic, was in town that day and escaped on one of the trains. She'd told Inga that the people who had enough time, enough foresight to pack a suitcase were forced to leave their bags behind at the depot to make room on the train for more passengers. Lisa and the McClains would have to carry or wear everything they wanted to take with them.

8

Chapter

Lisa and Mary were upstairs in Mary's bedroom sorting through the clothes and other items they'd piled on Mary's bed when they heard the front door open and slam against the foyer wall.

"Mary! Liisa!"

"Mama!" Mary cried heading for the stairs.

Mrs. McClain won her battle with the gale-like winds and managed to push the front door shut. Her hair—which earlier had been so carefully pulled back in a French knot —now looked like a ratty, used Brillo pad, with large tangled strands hanging in her face and down her back. Her eyes were red-rimmed and full of tears. From the top of the stairs, Lisa couldn't tell if it was the wind, or if Mrs. McClain was actually crying.

"White ash is falling like snow out there. We've got to go, girls. Did you find Michael?"

"Pedar's still out looking for him," Lisa said.

"Go where, Mama?" Mary asked, running down the stairs to hug her mother.

"Back to the depot. Mr. Fauley thinks he has enough cars and engines to put together four trains to take everyone out of town. He's pulling them together now. They should be ready to go in about an hour, and we're going to be on one of them."

"What about Papa?"

"Martin has decided to play captain and go down with his ship," Mrs. McClain said pushing a stray hair out of her eyes. "Believe me, I tried to talk some sense into him, but he's bound and determined to stay and try to save his precious mill."

Where were Pedar and Michael? If the trains weren't leaving for an hour, Lisa knew there was still time to get to safety, but all the same, she was feeling anxious to leave for the depot.

"Mary and I pulled together some things we thought you'd want to take, in case we had to leave," Lisa said to Mrs. McClain. "Mary picked out the clothes she wants, and we took clothes for you and Michael, and Mr. McClain, too—but you should look them over to make sure we've got the right things."

Mrs. McClain stared up the stairs at Lisa. "I don't know. I mean, I don't think that's really necessary. We'll only be gone a day. Once the fire's gone past us, we can come back tomorrow."

"But Mrs. McClain, what if you can't get back for a couple of days?" Lisa asked, trying hard to remember she was supposed to be a servant and couldn't be too pushy. "Better to be safe than sorry."

Mrs. McClain looked so tired, Lisa felt sorry for her. "Why don't you and Mary come upstairs and you can decide what you want to take. I'll help you pack."

"Come on, Mama, I'll show you what Liisa and I've got so far." Mary grabbed her mother's hand and began pulling her up the stairs.

"I guess it couldn't hurt to be prepared," Mrs. McClain said as her daughter led her into her bedroom. "Oh my goodness!"

Mary's bed was buried beneath a pile of clothes, books, hats, and other items, including two silver-framed photos, a pair of crystal candlesticks, a small black leather jewelry case, and a gold pocket watch with a chain.

"What is all this?!" Mrs. McClain exclaimed.

"We did get a little carried away," Lisa admitted. "You'll just have to choose the things you think can't be replaced, the things you can't live without."

"Now you're being melodramatic. Maybe a change of clothes . . . and yes, the family photo and our wedding photo. Thank you Mary, I wouldn't want to lose them. My black taffeta dress, I love that dress. And the fox muff I got from Martin for our anniversary last year. His grandfather's pocket watch, your father will want that."

Lisa was growing more and more impatient. A few minutes ago, Mrs. McClain had been raring to go. Now, she was picking over the items on the bed as if she had all the time in the world. "Mrs. McClain, you and Mary are going to have to wear as many clothes as you can. Layer them, one on top of the other. Pick practical clothes, warm clothes. We just have to find something to put the other things in. I don't think they'll let you take a suitcase on the train."

"We aren't going to be gone long enough that we'll need to pack a suitcase," Mrs. McClain said, looking at Lisa quizzically. "But I suppose it couldn't hurt to take some things just in case."

"Liisa, how about the aprons your mother made?" Mary asked. "You know, Mama, the one Liisa wears when she does laundry. She keeps the clothespins in the pockets. And the other one's in the kitchen on the hook by the pantry. They have really deep pockets, and we can wear them under our coats."

"Oh, honey, that's a great idea!" Mrs. McClain smiled at her daughter. "We could even baste the pockets shut, so we don't lose anything. The sewing basket's in my bedroom; I had to sew a button back on my coat this morning. I'll get it. Oh, I'm sorry Liisa, we didn't even ask you if we could borrow them. Would you mind? We'll get them back to you. And you still need to pack your own things."

Lisa nodded a silent okay and started for the stairs. For some reason, she knew exactly where Liisa's room was: on the first floor off the kitchen. Mary came clamoring down the stairs behind her.

"I'll get the aprons, Liisa. You get your things."

Lisa followed the now running Mary down the front hallway into the kitchen. She could see a small room to the left, a corner of a bed visible through the partially closed doorway. She pushed the door open. The room held only a bed and a dresser, but she saw immediately that she was in the right place; on the dresser, next to a faux tortoiseshell hairbrush and comb, was the familiar Maki family photo in a handmade, unvarnished pine frame. It confirmed what she'd been beginning to suspect. Inside, she was still Lisa Hanson; her own personality, her own memories had traveled through time with her. But the outside and some of her instincts, some of her feelings, were now Liisa Maki's. That explained the intensity of the feelings she felt for a young man she'd never met until a couple of hours ago.

Lisa picked up the picture frame and put it under her left arm. Clothes, she needed to find clothes. There wasn't a closet in the room, so everything must be in the dresser.

The top drawer held three pairs of underwear and two camisoles, all obviously homemade and hand-sewn, and one pair of stockings. The words " The Pillsbury Company" ran across the bottom of one pair of underwear, "Gold Medal" on another, and part of the Gold Medal medallion on the third pair. Flour sacks? She wondered what was printed on the pair she was wearing. The camisoles were made out of similar material, but either the printing had been bleached out, or they had been cut in such a way that the printed part of the sack had been avoided.

The middle drawer held two navy blue skirts, two white blouses, a crisp white apron, and a dress similar to the one she was wearing. The skirts, blouses, and apron must be her uniform for work.

Lisa shut the bedroom door, put the photo on the bed, and unbuttoned her dress. She took both camisoles from the drawer and put them on over the one she was already wearing. Then she lifted up the skirt of her dress and pulled on two of the bloomer-style pairs of underwear; four pairs would be too many and she'd need to be able to move.

She re-buttoned the dress, then pulled out one blouse and one skirt from the drawer, and put them on over the clothes she was wearing. A wool coat hung on a hook on the back of the bedroom door. Lisa took it down and slung it over her left arm. She put the pair of stockings in her left pocket, the hairbrush and comb in her right pocket, picked up the photo, and opened the door.

"Mrs. McClain, Mary, I've got all of my things. Is there anything else you need from down here? We should really start for the depot," Lisa called up the stairs.

"We'll be down in a minute. We're almost done," Mrs. McClain called back from upstairs.

Mary came down the stairs first, and Lisa—anxious as she was—had to turn her face away to keep from laughing. Even though the waistband had obviously been rolled over several times, the bottom of the apron still hung about two inches below the hem of her open coat.

"Mary, you're going to trip. What have you got in there?" Lisa asked, looking at the low-hanging apron.

"Well, I thought I'd better take my geography book so I can see where Matt's going when he gets better, and my piggy bank, and they're both pretty heavy. It's a good thing your mother made these aprons out of feedsacks. If they can hold 100 pounds of chicken feed, they should hold my things."

Helen Maki was obviously ahead of her time as far as recycling goes, Lisa thought as she noticed the words "Archer Brand Poultry Feeds—100 LBS Net" printed across the front of the apron. But with money so tight and a war going on, her great-grandmother had been forced to be creative with what few resources she had.

"I wish Michael would get here," Mrs. McClain said as she came down the stairs. "We've got to go. Maybe we should leave him a note telling him to meet us at the depot."

She still doesn't get it, Lisa thought. This house and everything in it is going to burn, including any note she leaves for Michael.

Lisa saw that Mrs. McClain was wearing her beloved black taffeta dress beneath a more practical blouse and skirt. Over that she wore a dark navy blue wool coat. Like Mary, the apron she wore was bulging with heavy items, and she was having some difficulty negotiating the stairs.

"Mama, why are you wearing your old coat? Your new one's so much nicer."

"And that's exactly why. I don't want to ruin my good coat with all the soot and smoke out there. I'm much better off wearing this old one. I don't care if I get it dirty."

I give up, Lisa thought. Mrs. McClain could wear her old coat and her best party dress, but that's all she'd have to wear for the next couple of weeks. Lisa had tried to tell her, but she realized she couldn't say too much more without raising suspicion.

Mrs. McClain stopped and put her hand on Lisa's arm as they met at the bottom of the stairs. "Something's been puzzling me, Liisa. Martin said you told him Mr. Fauley had some trains ready to get people out of town. How did you know? I know because I was at the depot, but how did you know?"

Lisa knew she had to think fast. "I saw Mr. Fauley talking to the Brookston train engineer. I knew if he thought Cloquet was in any danger, he'd make sure there were trains to take us all out of town."

Mrs. McClain looked at her as though she didn't quite accept that as a logical explanation, but her attention was quickly drawn to the sound of a car honking its horn outside.

"Is it Papa?" Mary asked, running to the window.

"I hope Martin's come to his senses and is going with us to the depot," Mrs. McClain said following her daughter to the window. "It's Martin's car, but Pedar's driving and he's got Michael with him. Thank God!"

Pedar and Michael got out of the car, both shielding their eyes with their hands from the wind-borne sand, leaves, and ash swirling outside. Mrs. McClain waited until they were on the porch and approaching the doorway before she opened the front door to let them in the house. Pedar and Michael both had to help her shut the door against the fierce wind.

"Michael!" Mrs. McClain said, grabbing her son by the shoulders and pulling him to her. "Where have you been? I've been so worried!"

"Jason and I started watching the fire come down the hill and we lost track of time," Michael said pulling back, his cheeks flushed red.

Lisa assumed he was embarrassed. Fifteen-year-old boys probably didn't like being hugged by their mothers in front of other people any more than fourteen-year-old girls did.

"They were standing on one of the board stacks off Eighth Street. Mr. McClain called the store and told me to come get his car to look for the boys. Once I found them, I gave Jason a ride home, and Michael and I came right here. I'm supposed to make sure you get to the depot and on a train."

"Thank you, Pedar. At least someone around here seems to have kept the sense God gave him." Mrs. McClain gave Michael a reproachful eye.

"I'm starving, what've we got to eat? Do we still have some of that ham from last night's dinner?" Michael asked.

Unbelievable! Lisa knew teenage boys were eating machines, but how could he think about stopping to eat now? "I brought biscuits back with me from the farm," she said, pointing at the cloth-covered tray on the chair near the phone, wanting to hurry things along.

"Great! I love your mother's biscuits!"

"Michael, I laid some clothes out for you, they're on your bed. Decide what you want to take with you; you're going to have to wear everything. See what Mary, Liisa, and I have done? While you're doing that, Liisa and I will make some sandwiches to take on the train. Come on, we should hurry. The trains will be leaving soon."

"Mrs. McClain, why don't you help Michael and I'll help Liisa. I think it'll go much faster if you go upstairs with Michael." Pedar smiled at Mrs. McClain, picked up the plate of biscuits and led Liisa towards the kitchen by her elbow.

"What about me? What can I do?" Mary asked trailing behind Liisa and Pedar.

"Liisa, you get the ham," Pedar said motioning towards a big wooden stand-alone cupboard with his hand. "Mary, you can show me where you keep the knives."

Wondering why last night's dinner was in the cupboard, Lisa walked towards it hesitantly. It had three doors, two short ones on the left and one long on the right. The door on the right was closest, so she opened it first.

Cold air hit her face as she saw that the ham was in there, along with some cheese and a couple bottles of milk. The cupboard's walls were lined with the same white enamel that covered the old chipped pots and pans Grandma Inga let her use in her sandbox when she was little, and the shelves were made of wire. She took out the ham and shut the cupboard door. Out of curiosity, she opened the top door on the left—the space inside was filled with a large block of ice. Instinctively, she shut the door quickly so the ice wouldn't melt, then shook her head in disbelief when she realized what she'd just done.

An icebox, Lisa thought in amazement as she carried the plate of ham over to the kitchen table. No wonder her grandma always called the refrigerator an icebox.

"I'll cut the ham, Liisa can slice the biscuits, and, Mary, you look for something to put the sandwiches in," Pedar said, taking charge again.

The three of them worked a small assembly line at the table. Pedar sliced the ham into thick quarter-inch slices, Liisa put a slice inside one of Helen's biscuits and secured it with a toothpick, then handed it off to Mary, who put the sandwich in the small flour sack that had covered the biscuits on their journey in the back of the wagon. Twelve biscuits, twelve sandwiches.

"Are you just about ready?" Mrs. McClain called from the foyer.

"We're coming," Pedar said putting what was left of the ham back in the icebox.

"I tried calling Martin at the mill to tell him we were leaving, but no one answered. The operators are calling everyone with a phone to tell them to get on the trains, and they've promised to try and get a hold of Martin and tell him we've left."

Mrs. McClain looked so lost and scared that Lisa's heart went out to her. Her oldest son had the Spanish flu, her husband was staying behind to fight a fire he had no chance of beating, and by tomorrow morning she would have no home and no clothes but the ones she was wearing. Plus, it was October. Winter was almost here. How, Lisa wondered, did these people get through this horrible thing?

"Mrs. McClain, I'll make sure the back door's locked. And if you'll give me the key to the front door, I'll lock it, too. Liisa, you get everybody out to the car." Pedar took the key from Mrs. McClain's outstretched hand and headed back towards the kitchen.

Michael opened the front door, and Lisa herded the McClains outside and towards the car. The wind was so strong, she had to lean forward to keep herself from being pushed backwards. Squinting her eyes to minimize contact with the wind-whirls of dirt and ash, Lisa could see Mrs. McClain ahead of her, holding tightly to her daughter's hand so the young girl wouldn't blow away. Michael opened the passenger-side front door and helped his mother in. Then he, Mary, and Lisa climbed into the back seat through the back door on the driver's side.

Pedar came out of the front door of the house, pulled it shut, and locked it. Head down, he fought his way to the driver's side of the car, opened the door, and slid behind the wheel.

"Wait! I forgot something!" Mary shouted over the noise of the wind. "I need to go back in the house."

"Mary!" they all cried in unison.

"Really. I need to go back. Pedar, give me the key."

"Okay," Pedar said after getting a reluctant nod from Mrs. McClain. "But I'm going with you. Hurry up." He opened the car door and helped Mary out. Still holding on to her hand, the two of them trudged up the walk and climbed the stairs to the front porch. Pedar opened the front door and he and Mary disappeared into the house.

The air was filled with smoke, and Lisa's eyes were stinging, her throat burning. What was taking them so long? Though it was probably no more than a few minutes, it seemed like ages before Pedar and Mary reappeared.

Pedar helped Mary into the back seat of the car before jumping into the driver's seat. The engine sputtered nervously, then roared to life just as a large branch from a birch tree near the curb broke off and crashed about a foot in front of the car.

"Go, go, go!" Lisa shouted, poking Pedar in the back with her finger. Pedar turned the wheels to avoid the branch, floored the accelerator, and drove purposefully over the center boulevard, saving time by skipping the turn-around at the end of Park Place, and headed the car back towards Vine Street. At the intersection with Chestnut, where Park Place turns into Avenue C, they encountered their first group of refugees trudging towards the depot.

"Pedar, it's Mrs. Wright and her granddaughter." Mrs. McClain pointed at an elderly woman carrying a young girl who looked around two or three years old. "We should give her a ride. She can't possibly carry that child all the way to the depot from here."

Pedar obligingly pulled the car to the side of the road. "We'll have to put the top down so that everybody will fit in the car."

"Fine. But we've got to help her," Mrs. McClain said back in her Red Cross mode. "Mrs. Wright, over here. Let us give you and your granddaughter a ride to the depot."

"Oh, Mrs. McClain, Pedar. Bless you. My husband's gone to help my daughter and her husband."

Pedar lowered the top of the car and strapped it down tight. Lisa shoved her picture frame down into the back waistband of her skirt so Mary could sit on her lap, and slid over next to Michael. Pedar helped Mrs. Wright and the little girl into the back seat, then climbed back behind the wheel and started the car.

"Ada twisted her ankle this morning," Mrs. Wright explained. "Plus, she's pregnant—due in three weeks—and my husband and son-in-law are trying to figure out a way to get her to the train since she can't put any weight on her right foot. We're supposed to meet them at the depot. Ada's daughter, Elsie, was staying with us this weekend. She's gotten so heavy, I'm having a hard time carrying her, but she can't walk in this wind."

"My God, it looks like Belgium!" Mrs. McClain said as they passed more people struggling towards the depot with suitcases and baby buggies full of belongings.

It did look like something from a movie or CNN. Though Lisa had no idea what Mrs. McClain was referring to, she assumed it had something to do with the war.

The smell of smoke was getting stronger, carrying with it a powerful sense of urgency. Elsie was hiding her face in her grandmother's shoulder, her arms tight around the older woman's neck. Lisa wished she had someone she could hold on to for reassurance.

Burning embers were now flying through the air, and with the top of the car folded down, one landed on Mary's lap. Mary and Lisa used their hands to beat out the smoldering glow on her coat. The next ember landed in Lisa's hair, and as she brushed it out, she momentarily regretted giving her scarf to Inga earlier.

Lisa looked at Elsie and wondered about her own grandmother. Was her family safe? Had they gone into the gravel pit? Again, Lisa worried that her being here could change history. She'd seen enough movies to know that bad things always happened when people tried to change history. All three *Back to the Future* and the first two *Terminator* movies were testaments to what could happen. On the other hand, the storyline of *Terminator 3* implied that things that were meant to happen will happen, whether you try to change them or not.

But this wasn't a movie, and Lisa no longer believed it was just a dream. What was she supposed to do? There was no way she could stop this fire, or stop the town from burning. Why was she here? It was all so unbelievable, so confusing, but she expected the answer would become clear. After all, everything happened for a reason.

"Mary, what was so important that you had to go back for it?" Lisa asked.

"I forgot my script."

The incredulity Lisa felt must have showed on her face. "I had to get my script for the school play," Mary said patting the apron inside in her coat. "I've got one of the lead roles, and I don't have all my lines memorized yet."

Abandoned cars and wagons made it impossible for Pedar to drive all the way up to the depot. He parked the car about a block away on Vine Street, and helped Mrs. McClain and Mrs. Wright out of the car. Lisa, Mary, and Michael climbed into the street and stepped directly into chaos.

People were converging on the depot, crowding to get on the trains. Horses, unharnessed once they'd delivered their owners to the depot, darted up and down the street, shrieking in fright from the smoke and flying, flaming debris. Baby buggies lined the depot platform, which was piled high with luggage. Like the people on the Brookston train earlier, the Cloquet refugees seemed to be in shock, walking like robots, mechanically, silently, towards the depot from all parts of town.

"I'll carry Elsie, if she'll let me," Pedar offered. The little girl whimpered and clung to her grandmother—no amount of persuasion could shake her from the older woman's arms. Mrs. Wright shifted her precious load to her left hip, and began walking with the others.

Holding tightly to a hand of each, Mrs. McClain walked determinedly between her two children, fighting the angry wind, as Pedar and Lisa brought up the rear of their little group.

"Liisa, look out!"

Out of the corner of her eye, Lisa saw something flying towards her. Pedar gave her right shoulder such a hard shove that she nearly tripped over her long skirt. A flaming board dropped from the sky and hit the street, sparks bouncing and lighting the grass along the curb on fire. Pedar rushed over and stomped out the flames with his boots.

Lisa's heart was pounding. It would have hit her if Pedar hadn't pushed her out of its path. He'd saved her life!

"What was that?" Lisa gasped, as Pedar grabbed her arm and began pulling her again towards the depot. "Where did it come from?"

"Come on. I promised Mr. McClain I'd get all of you on the train."

They caught up with the McClains on the depot platform. A passenger train was first in line and rapidly taking on passengers.

"Sorry, Ma'am," a man said, stopping a woman trying to board the train with a large suitcase. "I'm afraid you'll have to leave it here. There's not enough room for all the people, let alone luggage."

"Please. My things. I need my things," she pleaded.

"Sorry, Ma'am," he repeated firmly. "No luggage. You'll have to leave it here with everyone else's."

The woman began to sob as she threw her suitcase on the pile of luggage, and climbed aboard. Mrs. McClain gave Lisa another "how did you know?" look. Lisa pretended not to understand.

"Michael, Mary, get on the train. Liisa, you too." Mrs. McClain pushed her children towards the stairs at the end of one of the passenger cars.

"Only women and children on this train. All men and boys over sixteen stay back to fight the fire," the man said, putting an arm in front of Michael.

"He's only fifteen, and he's coming with us." Mrs. McClain pushed the man's arm aside. "Mrs. Wright, you and Elsie must get on this train."

"No, we've got to wait for my husband and my daughter. We'll get on the next train." Mrs. Wright turned away from the train and looked up Vine Street. "How are they going to get Ada down here? She can't walk. What if she goes into labor?" The poor woman looked close to crumbling.

"I'll go back and get her with the car, if that's okay with you?" Pedar looked at Mrs. McClain. "They won't let me on anyway, and I promised Mr. McClain I'd get you on a train and out of town. If I pick them up with the car, I can get them back here in time to catch another train."

"Yes. Good idea, Pedar. Go get them, then you get on the train with them. I don't care if you have to lie and tell them you're only fifteen, you get on a train. Come on, Liisa. All the seats will be taken and we'll have to stand." Reaching down from the passenger car stairs where she stood, Mrs. McClain held her hand out towards Lisa who was still on the depot platform.

"I'm going with Pedar," she heard herself say. The minute the words were out of her mouth, she realized this was how and where Liisa and the McClains had parted company, and why they didn't know what happened to her. It was more than wanting to be with Pedar; she knew somehow that this was something she had to do.

"Are you crazy? I don't need your help, I need you to get on that train!" Pedar said, pushing her towards Mrs. McClain's outstretched hand.

"Liisa, get on this train!" Mrs. McClain shouted over the shrieks of the mill whistles, which were now going off with a furor. Suddenly the train let out an ear-piercing whistle of its own and began to pull out of the station.

Mrs. McClain grabbed the stair railing to keep her balance, and leaned out, looking back at Lisa as the train began to pull away. "Liisa!" she cried. "What will I tell your mother?"

"I'll be fine. You take care of Mary and Michael," she yelled back, then turned to Mrs. Wright. "Don't worry, we'll get your daughter here."

"I promised Mr. McClain I'd get everyone on the train, and that means you, too. You missed that train, but you're going to be on the next one. Do you hear me?" Pedar's face had turned pink, and Lisa half-expected to see steam coming out of his ears at any time.

She ignored him, and instead turned to Mrs. Wright and asked her for the address of her daughter's house. "Pedar and I will take the McClain's car, get your family, and bring them here. You'll all be able to leave together."

Lisa knew, deep in her heart she knew, she was not supposed to get on that train. And, most important of all, she felt she was getting closer, so much closer to finding out what had really happened to her great-aunt, Liisa Maki.

Chapter

edar wouldn't even look at Lisa. They'd both run to the car, but he'd almost sprinted, as if hoping to lose her in the crowd, willing her back to the depot and on a train. Her heavy, long skirts had slowed her down, but she'd finally caught up with him. Now, as they drove towards Mrs. Wright's daughter's house, Pedar acted as though she wasn't there.

She hated that he was mad at her. Lisa wished she could explain, make him understand, but what could she say?

"Pedar, this morning I fell asleep as Lisa Hanson, and when I woke up, it was 1918. Everyone thought I was my great-aunt, Liisa Maki, who disappeared today, the day of the Cloquet Fire. Liisa Maki didn't get on that train with the McClains, and somehow I just know she stayed behind with you. For our family's sake, but most of all, for my grandma's sake, I need to find out why. I need to find out what happened to her."

Right, and then he'd have her committed. Pedar already thought she was acting strangely; there'd be no doubt in his mind that she was crazy if she told him the truth. What did they do with crazy people in 1918? She didn't think the psychiatric hospital in Moose Lake was open yet, and even if it were, this fire would consume the town of Moose Lake, too.

"Pedar," she said, "I'm sorry I've made you mad, but I have to do this. I can't tell you why; I'm not really sure myself, but trust me, I need to go with you." Lisa looked at the young man behind the wheel, his usually smiling face was stern and still very pink.

"Liisa, I've got more important things to do than watch out for you. If anything happens to you, I . . ." He left the sentence hanging.

"What? You'll be in trouble with the McClains, with my family? You're not responsible for me, Pedar. I can make my own decisions." It was obvious now, he thought of her as a child. That hurt. She was only fourteen and he was going to be eighteen next week, but she'd been thinking, been hoping that he felt the same about her as she did about him.

The silence was stifling, smothering, and magnified by the sudden absence of the mill sirens. Lisa couldn't breathe. Was it the smoke or her fight with Pedar that was the problem?

"Well," Pedar said, finally cracking the wall between them. "You were right about Cloquet burning. I suppose you could be right about this, too."

"What do you mean?" Lisa asked. This wasn't the reaction she'd expected at all.

"Earlier, when the Brookston train came in, you said Cloquet was going to burn, too. I told you the fire department would build a firebreak and stop the fire before it reached us. I was wrong. That board that almost hit you was from Bottle Alley. The whole thing must be on fire. The wind is strong enough now that it's lifting those burning boards and dropping them all over town, starting fires everywhere they land. We can't build a firebreak against the wind, and our little fire department can't be everywhere at once. Cloquet's going to burn, isn't it? The whole town will be gone."

Could she, should she tell him the truth, the real truth? No, she didn't dare, and what was the truth anyway?

"Yes," Lisa said, "I believe it is."

Neither of them said anything until Pedar pulled the car up in front of a small white clapboard house on the east side of Twelfth Street. "We're going to help get Ada on a train, and you're getting on with her. No arguments, okay?"

"As long as you get on the train with me," Lisa said.

She heard him mumbling something under his breath as they climbed the front porch stairs; the only word she could make out was "stubborn." She smiled in spite of her growing anxiety. Her Grandma Inga and her mother had called her the same thing many times.

Pedar knocked on the front door and called out, "Mr. Wright, Charles. It's Pedar Oleson. I've got a car. We're here to help you get Ada to the train."

The front door swung open. "Thank God you're here, Pedar. Charles and I've been trying to build a litter to carry Ada down to Johnson's Crossing. The operators called and said the trains were stopping there to pick up passengers who couldn't make it to the depot."

"Mr. Wright, can you and Charles carry your daughter to the car? We should be able to sit her the long way in the back seat."

"Charles? Dad? Who's at the door?" a woman's voice called from a room towards the back of the house.

Lisa heard a door in the back of the house open and close, and a younger man in his late twenties came running down the hallway.

"Charles, Pedar's here," Mr. Wright said to his son-in-law. "He's got a car. Get Ada ready. We're leaving."

"What can we do to help?" Lisa asked, stepping into the house.

Charles came out of the back room carrying his wife in his arms. The very pregnant, very tired-looking woman was wearing a light green dress, but both feet were bare; her right ankle the color of eggplant, bruised and swollen.

Smiling wanly at Pedar, she thanked him for coming, and asked how he knew they needed help. That smile sent a small stab of jealousy through Lisa's chest, and she noticed the color of Ada's dress contrasted perfectly with her auburn hair and set off her eyes, which were an unusually bright green with brown flecks that glowed like gold. There was no denying the woman was beautiful, and Lisa felt an irrational inclination to dislike her without knowing her or anything about her.

"We saw your mother and Elsie on their way to the depot and gave them a ride," Pedar answered. "She told us

Charles and your father were trying to find a way to get you to the train. Mrs. McClain offered her car, so here we are."

"You took Mom and Elsie to the depot? Did they get on a train?"

"Your mother wanted to wait for your father. But I'm sure they're okay." Pedar smiled back at her. "Now we just need to get you on a train." He gave Charles a friendly pat on the back and nodded towards the car outside. Charles looked back at his father-in-law, then carried his wife through the front door, all the while telling her everything was going to be okay, though he didn't sound too sure himself.

Did Pedar know everyone in town?

"She'll need a coat, some warm clothes," Lisa said to Mr. Wright, feeling just a little guilty for disliking a woman she didn't even know. "Something for her feet. At least some stockings. How about a quilt or a blanket?"

"In the bedroom." Mr. Wright pointed to the room his daughter and son-in-law had come out of, then turned to follow them out the door.

Lisa ran to the back bedroom. She found a quilt on the bed and another one on a shelf in the closet. She took them both and a pillow off the bed. Lisa was headed towards the dresser to see if she could find some socks for Ada, when Pedar came rushing into the room carrying some wet towels in his hands.

"Liisa, what's taking so long?" he asked.

"She needs something for her feet."

"She won't be walking anywhere. The quilts should be enough to keep her warm."

Pedar grabbed the other pillow off the bed and he and Lisa ran out of the house and into the car. This time, he didn't even bother to shut the front door, let alone lock it.

The two men were already sitting in the back seat with Ada stretched across their laps, her head resting on her husband's chest, eyes closed. Lisa threw one of the quilts over Ada, but kept the other one and the two pillows on her lap. Pedar handed her the towels and started the car, made a U-turn, and headed north on Twelfth Street back towards Cloquet Avenue.

"Ada and Charles need to get on the first train that stops at Johnson's Crossing," Mr. Wright said to Pedar. "She should see a doctor as soon as possible. If you're going back to the depot, I'll go with you and get Edna and Elsie. We'll just have to meet up with Ada and Charles later."

Though the sun had long gone down, the encroaching fire lit up the night sky, making it seem almost as bright as midday and casting an eerie, orange reflection on the surrounding houses and trees. To the west, they could see embers and flaming pinecones flying through the air, lighting the tops of trees and telephone poles on fire. The fire was coming their way, but hadn't reached the east end of town, where they were, yet.

Even so, Lisa could feel her adrenaline kick into gear, her heart trying to beat a path out of her chest. At Cloquet Avenue, Pedar turned right. The depot was left. He must be going to Johnson's Crossing, thought Lisa. She'd never heard of it and had no idea where it was, which made her even more anxious.

As it turned out, Johnson's Crossing was the railroad crossing near the intersection of Cloquet Avenue and Fourteenth Street. A large crowd had gathered to catch the next train, and Pedar drove as near to the crossing as he could.

"This is as close as I can get, you're going to have to carry her the rest of the way." Pedar turned to look at Charles in the back seat. "Can you make it?"

"I think so. Thank you so much. Jacob, are you going back to the depot with them?"

"Yes. I've got to find Edna and Elsie," Mr. Wright said. "You take care of Ada and the baby, that's what's important. I'll leave word with my brother in Duluth, he'll know where to find us. You let him know where you are so we can find you."

Mr. Wright slid out of the back seat, and helped Charles lift his wife out of the car.

"We should at least stay until the train comes. He can't stand holding her like that for very long," Lisa said to Pedar. "Even though she's small, she's almost nine months pregnant."

"Liisa's right, Charles," Pedar said. "We'll stay here until the next train comes. You and Ada should wait in the car."

As if on cue, a train whistle sounded. The train was coming. Lisa got out of the car, carrying the two pillows. "We'll help you get your wife on the train," she said to Charles. "These pillows should make her more comfortable."

The train pulled slowly into the crossing. Unlike the passenger train the McClains boarded, this train was a mix of boxcars and open ore gondolas pulled by a small switch engine.

"Everyone gets on. Make room. This is the last train," shouted a man jumping down from the engine. He wore a big fur coat and seemed to be in charge.

Pedar and Lisa looked at each other, and then at Mr. Wright.

"Chief McSweeney, is there anyone still down at the depot? My wife and granddaughter were waiting for me there."

The police chief looked at Mr. Wright, but continued assisting people into one of the gondolas. "There's no one there Jacob. Everyone got on a train. I didn't see which one Edna got on, but she has to be on one of them. The depot's on fire, Jacob. We've got to get out of here."

Lisa felt Pedar's hand on her back, pushing her towards one of the gondolas.

"Liisa, you're getting on this train."

"Then so are you." Lisa turned to face Pedar. "We had a deal."

"Please, give my wife some room. She's got to stretch out her leg," they heard Charles pleading. "Don't step on her. Ada, are you all right?"

"Well, it looks like we're needed in this car," Lisa said grabbing Pedar's arm and moving towards the young couple's boxcar.

The last couple of boxcars on this final train had started on fire before the train pulled out from the depot. While the passengers managed to beat the flames out with coats and blankets, many of the frightened refugees had moved to the more crowded boxcars and the open-topped ore gondolas closer to the front of the train. Pedar discovered a boxcar carrying only eight people towards the back of the train, and brought his party back to it, away from the standing-room-only cars up front.

Concentrating on the situation at hand, Pedar and Lisa spread one of the quilts out on the floor of the dusty, dirty boxcar for Ada as if they were having a picnic, instead of fleeing for their lives. Charles lovingly lifted her into the arms of her father inside the car, who set her down as gently as possible on the quilt. It was only after they had Ada settled in, one pillow placed between her back and the wall of the boxcar, and the other pillow folded in half, her swollen ankle resting on top of it, that Lisa had a chance to observe her fellow passengers.

Rich and poor, young and old, no one had been spared the trauma of this night. Their boxcar held a young mother with a baby and two small children; an elderly couple holding each other and talking and crying in Finnish; two young men in their early twenties; and last but far from least, a woman in her mid-fifties who sat center stage holding a bird cage containing a big yellow and green parrot on her lap.

Just before the train finally pulled out, an enterprising refugee attempted to board their boxcar with two goats in tow. Chief McSweeney saw her, and even though there was obviously room in the boxcar, he told her in no uncertain terms that the goats weren't allowed. In a thick Swedish accent, the woman pleaded with the police chief, but to no avail. The chief stood firm, the goats stayed behind, and the human priority was maintained.

"If this train is only for people, why does she get to bring that?" the woman asked, pointing at the woman with the parrot.

Lisa wasn't sure if the "goat lady" was referring to the parrot or the large suitcase the woman was sitting on, but the woman with the parrot wrapped her arms tightly around the cage in her lap as if daring anyone to take it from her. The question was rhetorical, but Lisa had to wonder what things the woman had left behind just so she could save her bird.

The train started with a jerk, and Lisa realized she'd been holding her breath—both from anxiety and to take in as little of the smoke billowing into the car as possible. She wished she could "blink" everyone to safety, like Barbara Eden in *I Dream of Jeannie*. Instead, the small switch engine strained to pull its load of refugee-filled boxcars and ore gondolas, and even when it was moving at its top speed, the train seemed to creep rather than chug along the tracks.

The heat from the burning grass and trees felt like a blast furnace, searing Lisa's face and licking her nostrils; the smoke scorching her throat and stinging her eyes.

Charles pulled a knife out of a sheath on his belt and cut the wet towels Lisa had carried onboard into quarters, handing a section each to Ada and Lisa, then passing them out to the others in the car. The wet towel made breathing much easier. Thank God Pedar had thought to bring them.

Her eyes fell on the young mother sitting on an over-turned wooden bucket, rocking her small baby wrapped tightly in a blue blanket; it couldn't have been more than a couple months' old. A boy around four and a girl around two sat quietly on the floor at her feet. The girl wore only one shoe, and a tiny pink toe poked through a hole in the dirty off-white stocking on her other foot. The whole family appeared to be in shock. Where was the father? The little girl started to cough, and her older brother gallantly showed her how to breathe through the wet towel.

"That poor woman with the children—she looks so scared," Lisa whispered to Ada.

"That's Mrs. Holmstrand. Her husband works for the railroad, and he's been out of town all week. She must be worried sick, wondering where he is, if he's all right," Ada said, her voice catching.

Lisa looked at Ada and saw that same fear and worry shadowed her face like a veil. Mrs. Wright and Elsie. Of course! She was worried about them. The irrational jealousy and initial dislike that Lisa felt for Ada when they first met evaporated under the intense glare of human compassion—and more guilt, knowing that her family would survive the fire. Well, almost everyone in her family; she still didn't know what had happened to Liisa.

"I'm sure they're okay—your mother and Elsie. They're on one of the trains. You heard what Chief McSweeney said; there wasn't anyone left back at the depot."

Ada nodded silently, and Lisa thought that maybe if she got Ada talking, she could keep her mind off her mother and daughter.

"Do you know any of the other people in our car?"

Apparently that was like asking if strawberries were red or the sky blue. Ada, it seemed, knew just about everything about everyone in town.

"Those two young men over there are brothers, Jalmer and Reino, who work with Charles at the mill. They're Finnish citizens and can't be drafted, but they were one of the first to buy liberty bonds because they love America, and don't want to be called slackers."

Lisa almost laughed, though she could see that Ada was quite serious. She'd just never heard anyone use the word "slacker" in a sentence before, and she had no idea what liberty bonds were, but she didn't want to show her ignorance by asking questions.

Ada didn't know the older couple, but it looked like they'd left in a hurry. Neither of them had coats, and the poor woman was wearing only a flimsy old housedress. The goat lady was Mrs. Sorenson—she was a cook for the boarding house on Sixth Street—and the lady with the parrot was Mrs. Oswald.

"You must know her," Ada insisted, "she's one of the McClains' neighbors."

Mrs. Oswald stood out in the boxcar; not just because there were only fourteen other people in the car, or because she had the parrot. The woman wore a fancy gold and green velvet evening gown, a black felt hat with a wide brim and a big white feather, and one of those hideous fur stoles that still had the heads and tails on it. She could have been on the cover of a *Glamour* "fashion don't" special issue.

"I've never seen her before," Lisa said truthfully, her first chance to say anything since Ada had begun to talk. "I think I'd remember if I had." How did Ada know Liisa worked for the McClains? Pedar obviously knew Charles and Ada; was it possible that Liisa knew them too?

While the two women talked, Charles, Pedar, and Mr. Wright stood in the open doorway of the boxcar with Jalmer and Reino, watching Mother Nature put on the show of her life. Hot embers and flaming pinecones continued to fly through the air, lighting rooftops, trees, and telephone poles ablaze from the top down as the train maintained its crawl. And then suddenly—in what seemed like the middle of nowhere—the train stopped.

13 Chapter

What was happening? Why had they stopped? Lisa could hear people shouting from the other train cars. The older couple in their car clung to each other, petrified, and the young mother with the baby hugged her two older children close.

"I'm going to find out what's going on," Charles said to Ada from the boxcar's doorway. "I'll be right back."

"I'll just stay here with Liisa," his wife joked, but Lisa could see in the firelight that her face was drained of all color.

Charles and Pedar jumped out of the boxcar and ran towards the front of the train. Though it seemed like hours, they were actually back in less than ten minutes. The depot agent, Mr. Fauley, was sitting on the cowcatcher, they reported, acting as a lookout for the engineer and holding a lantern to help light the way through the thick fog-like smoke. He'd spotted some burning trees on the tracks ahead, and once they were cleared away, the train would start moving again.

"Pedar and I have offered to help clear the tracks if we have to stop again," Charles told Ada as he sat down next to her on the quilt. His wife didn't respond, but grabbed Lisa's hand with a vice grip that nearly broke her fingers. Lisa felt the same heavy concern rise like bile in her throat, and looked over at Pedar, who stood again, nonchalantly, near the doorway of the boxcar.

"If you don't want me to, I won't." Charles looked at Ada, who mercifully loosened her grip, but continued holding onto Lisa's hand.

"I can't get you to move a sack of potatoes, but you volunteer to clear away trees that are on fire?"

"I told you I'd bring the potatoes down into the root cellar, and I would have. You should've waited for me to get home, instead of trying to bring them down those stairs yourself, especially now. You're going to have a baby in a couple weeks."

"I admit it wasn't the best idea I've ever had." Ada looked at her swollen ankle, resting precariously on the pillow in front of her. "But I'm not so sure this is such a great idea either. Charles, I'm scared."

"Don't worry," Charles picked up his wife's other hand and kissed it, "we'll be careful."

The next two times the train stopped, Pedar, Charles, and the two young men jumped out of the boxcar and headed up front, and Mr. Wright joined Ada and Lisa on the quilt. Both times the men were back within twenty minutes, sweaty, dirty, and full of soot. The third time, the train stopped midway on a high trestle bridge across a river. Ada's hand tightened around Lisa's as the men again descended onto the tracks, Mr. Wright joining them this time. Even the parrot must have felt the suffocating fear that seemed to suck all of the air out of the boxcar, as it began to flap its wings and squawk, "shut up!" over and over again.

Through the open boxcar door Lisa could see the front part of the train where it curved onto the bridge. The wooden trestle looked so skeletal, so flimsy; it reminded her of the latticework trellis in their neighbor's garden. She couldn't believe it could hold any train, let alone this train filled beyond normal capacity.

Though it was probably no more than thirty minutes, it seemed like hours since the men had left. What were they doing? Why was it taking them so long this time? Lisa was afraid to look, afraid of what she might see, but felt the same compelling need as drivers who slow down to gawk at an accident on the freeway.

With Ada's hand still clamped around hers, she couldn't move closer to the doorway, so Lisa craned her neck to get a better look at the front of the train. Men were hosing down the tracks, using water stored in the switch engine. Were the tracks actually on fire? Would they be able to cross this bridge? If not, would the train have to back up? Then what?

Ada knew Lisa could see what was happening up front, but she was obviously too afraid to ask. Instead, she continued to talk about people she knew, about the town, giving Lisa a personal tour of Cloquet no history book could ever give her. Lisa had opened the floodgates when she'd started Ada talking to take her mind off her missing mother and daughter. Now with her increased nervousness over the men's long absence, it was as though the dam had broken wide open.

"Poor Mrs. Swedberg. Her son Carl's casket came in on the train this morning and was delivered to his mother's house for the funeral tomorrow. It's bad enough that her son died of influenza during training at Camp Grant, but now she can't even give him a real burial. With the way the west end was lit up, her house and her son are both lost."

Lisa sat and listened quietly while Ada talked, nodding occasionally when she felt Ada needed some kind of response.

"You know Ole Kolseth's general store burned down last Good Friday. He just finished rebuilding on the same corner, and he and his family spent all day stocking shelves, getting ready for their Grand Opening on Monday. He has nine children, Liisa. If this new store burns, he's going to have to rebuild again. How will they make a living, how will they eat in the meantime? How will any of us live?"

Ada's voice had become barely a whisper, and Lisa felt compelled to reassure her new friend.

"Cloquet will rebuild," she said. "The town and the jobs will come back."

"I hope you're right, Liisa. I believe God has a plan for all of us. Everything happens for a reason, though it may not always make sense at the time. Pedar goes to our church, that's how we know him," Ada said, eerily echoing her Grandma Inga's belief, and unknowingly answering a question that had been bothering Lisa since they'd first arrived at the Swansons'. "Did you know Pedar before you started riding with him to visit your family?"

"How…?"

"I know you ride with him every other Saturday. He's talked about you quite a few times."

"He has? What did he say?" That explained how Ada knew she worked for the McClains, but Lisa was more than just surprised, shocked actually, that Pedar talked about her to Ada. Especially since he'd made it clear he saw her as a child, not the young woman she felt she was.

Before Ada could answer, the train lurched forward, and began a slow, jerking crawl. The men weren't back yet! Pulling her hand from Ada's, Lisa scrambled up from the quilt and ran to the doorway, looking toward the front of the train.

"Do you see them?" Ada called.

Lisa nodded. She could see all five men running along the edge of the trestle bridge towards their car. The train was moving slowly enough that when their boxcar reached them, the men climbed onboard with little effort. They'd been gone over forty-five minutes this time.

"What took you so long?"

"Are you all right?"

Ada and Lisa bombarded them with questions, grateful they all appeared to be fine, angry that they'd been made to worry.

The tracks on the bridge had been too hot to hold the train, Charles told the women, and they had to hose them down and allow them to cool before the train could travel over the trestle. It had taken much longer than anyone expected, but everything was fine.

Drenched in sweat and covered with soot and ash, the men took their places in the boxcar doorway, this time sitting rather than standing. They were obviously spent, exhausted from their recent ordeal. As if he knew Lisa was thinking about him, still worried about him, Pedar turned his head to look back at her. She smiled to let him know everything was fine, and he returned to watching the inferno rage along the tracks.

If Ada and Grandma Inga were right, and everything happens for a reason, what am I doing here? Lisa wondered. Along with the rest of her family, she'd always wanted to know what had happened to her great-aunt Liisa, and now she was about to find out. Is that why she was here?

Suddenly it hit her. Whatever had happened to Liisa was going to happen to her. It was like knowing something was going to happen in an action-thriller movie, but not knowing what or when, so you sat on the edge of your seat, holding your breath through the whole film.

Could Liisa have died and been misidentified, or possibly been hurt and gotten amnesia? Lisa remembered the story of her Grandpa John's sister, Hilda, who suffered a head injury when she fell off the roof of their house while the family was trying to keep it wet during the fire. Family history said she was never the same. She'd died before Lisa was even born.

How much longer? Lisa wondered. Carlton was certainly less than ten miles away, and yet they'd been on this train for over two hours.

"Ow!" Pedar suddenly shouted, putting a hand over his right eye. "Something just flew in my eye."

As Lisa started to stand up to go see if she could help him, Ada grabbed her arm.

"Liisa," she said much too calmly, "my water just broke."

S hocked by Ada's announcement, Lisa blurted out the first thing that popped into her head, "I don't know nuthin' 'bout birthin babies, Miss Scarlett."

Gone with the Wind was her mother's favorite movie. She owned the video and whenever Butterfly McQueen said that line, Lisa's mother, her sisters, and Lisa would all say it with her. It seemed like a natural response.

But the bewildered look on Ada's face instantly told Lisa she'd made another mistake. She knew the movie came out in the late '30s, but she wasn't sure when the book had been printed. Obviously not yet, or if it had, Ada hadn't read it. The humor in the reference, however small, was completely lost on her, and Lisa realized she needed to change the subject, quickly.

"How long have you been having contractions?" she asked.

"I've been having small ones since before you and Pedar came and got us. I didn't tell Charles—he's nervous enough as it is. But they're getting stronger. I'm so afraid I'm going to have the baby here." Ada's eyes swept the dirty, rough floorboards of the boxcar.

"What can I do? Do you want me to get Charles or your father?" Lisa asked.

"Pedar said your youngest brother is only five. You must have helped your mother when he was born. You can help me, if it comes to that, can't you?"

Liisa Maki would have been nine when Arvo was born, old enough to have been some help during a home birth. But Lisa Hanson was the youngest of three girls, and all she knew about babies being born was what she'd seen on TV or in the movies—and, for some reason no one ever explained, you needed boiling water, lots and lots of boiling water.

"I'm sorry Ada, but my job was to watch the other kids," Lisa improvised, thinking it sounded like a believable excuse. "I really don't know anything about delivering babies. But I'll do whatever you tell me to."

There wasn't much she could do but wait and try to make Ada as comfortable as possible. Every so often, Charles, Pedar, or Mr. Wright would look their way, and the two women would smile and nod to assure them everything was fine.

It was close to 1:00 AM by the time the train finally pulled into Carlton, and Ada's contractions were getting closer and closer together. Men carrying lanterns and women with blankets swarmed the depot platform, offering their assistance and their homes to the Cloquet refugees. Though she didn't know much about labor, Lisa knew the first thing they had to do was find was a doctor for Ada. Charles seemed to have the same idea. He jumped out of the car before the train had come to a complete stop, and started asking everyone in the crowd where he could find a doctor, unaware that the situation had actually become urgent.

Pedar and Mr. Wright came over to help Ada out of the boxcar, and Lisa saw for the first time that Pedar's right eye lid was swollen at least three times its normal size. The right side of his face had always been in the shadows when Lisa and Ada had seen him checking on them from their corner of the boxcar.

"Pedar! Your eye!" Lisa exclaimed. "Can you even open it?"

"No," Pedar said. "When Charles brings the doctor back, I'll have him look at it."

"I'm in labor, Dad," Ada was saying to her father, but hearing the shock in Lisa's voice, she turned to look at Pedar. "My God, Pedar, aren't we a pretty pair!"

"The doctor's up to his elbows in people with burns," Charles said rushing up to the door of the boxcar, slightly out of breath from running. "His nurse said that unless it's an emergency, we should get on the passenger train that's going to Superior."

"She's in labor, Charles," Lisa said. "You don't have time to make the trip to Superior."

"Ada? How long have you..? Why didn't you tell me?" Charles stammered in surprise.

"Charles, wherever that doctor is, we need to go now," Ada puffed, wincing at the piercing intensity of her current contraction.

"Here, put her in this," Mr. Wright said, pushing an old, rusty, dented wheelbarrow that had obviously seen better days up to the side of the boxcar. Lisa hadn't even noticed that he'd gone.

"Pedar needs to see the doctor, too," she said, looking again at his swollen eye. "Does it hurt?"

"Yes," Pedar said. "But right now Ada needs to see a doctor more than I do."

Mr. Wright folded the quilt Ada and Lisa had been sitting on in the boxcar so that the wet section was on the bottom, and placed it in the wheelbarrow. Lisa lay the pillows on top of the quilt, as Charles lifted his wife out of the boxcar and put her in the make-do stretcher.

Charles hurriedly pushed the wheelbarrow through the crowd of confusion—refugees trying to find family members who had ended up on different train cars, Carlton hosts offering their homes for the evening, Red Cross nurses performing triage for the two doctors overwhelmed with smoke, burn, and shock victims.

"Please help us. My wife's having a baby," Charles called to a nurse bandaging the arm of a young boy about ten years old, his cheeks stained with soot and tears.

The nurse looked up quickly, and pointed down the street. "Over there. The gray house with the porch light on. Doctor Shepard's taking the emergencies."

Charles turned the wheelbarrow to the right, and pushed it across the street and up the front walk of the gray house. A nurse opened the front door and poked her head out. "What do we have?" she asked

Charles told her Ada was in labor.

"Come on in. I'll get the doctor."

Lisa ran up the steps and held the door open for Charles as he carried Ada into the house. Pedar and Mr. Wright followed. The nurse led them through the living room crowded with weary, dirty men, women, and children needing urgent medical attention and into a bedroom down the hall. Charles lay Ada on the bed as the doctor came into the room, wiping his hands on a towel.

"Quite a night to remember, Mrs...?"

"Swanson. Mrs. Charles Swanson," Ada answered breathlessly. "Doctor, this is my second baby. I don't think it's going to be much longer."

"Okay. I need to examine Mrs. Swanson, so why don't you all move to the other room. I'll ask the nurse to take a look at your eye," the doctor said, looking at Pedar.

The nurse led them back out to the living room. There was no place to sit; people already were on every chair or sitting on the floor, some crying, some quietly in shock, and some trying to comfort others. A girl around ten years old, her golden curls covered with bits of leaves and ashes, was having a splint put on her arm in one chair. In another, a nurse was stitching up a gash on the forehead of a young mother holding her crying toddler on her lap. The room was so full of people, Lisa couldn't tell who needed medical attention, and who was waiting for family or friends; everyone looked like they needed help. Only the nurses in their starched white Red Cross uniforms played obvious roles.

Outside of a few weddings and funerals, Lisa had never seen adults cry before. The true horror of the situation enveloped her and tears began to well in her own eyes. These people had lost everything but the clothes on their backs. This wasn't just a family story anymore, or a chapter in one of her history books.

Pedar was explaining to a nurse that something had blown into his eye over an hour earlier, and now he couldn't open it. The nurse said that the best she could do for him here was flush it with saline and put a bandage over it. He'd be better off taking the passenger train to Superior. There were more doctors and more medical supplies there.

On the road again, Lisa thought, as she and Pedar exchanged knowing looks. If Liisa had made it to Superior, what had happened to her once she got there? And why, she suddenly realized, had none of the family stories included anything about Pedar?

The passenger train's whistle announced its impending departure as Pedar and Lisa climbed aboard. Lisa spotted an empty seat near the front of the car, and pointed it out to Pedar. They'd barely had time to say goodbye to Ada, Charles, and Mr. Wright, and Lisa felt terrible about leaving her new friend in the middle of labor, not knowing how she and the baby were doing.

The winds had shifted and Carlton would be spared Cloquet's devastating fate. Many people had taken refuge with Carlton families. Those with serious injuries or emergency medical situations, like Ada, stayed at Dr. Shephard's make-do hospital. This train was filled with walking wounded, more emotionally than physically scarred by the previously unimaginable events of the past evening.

Trying to find a comfortable position on the hard seat, Lisa's back and legs ached with a tiredness she'd never felt before. It seemed so long ago, and yet she'd been just getting home from school and coming down with the flu only hours earlier. Was she still sleeping, dreaming in her bed at home, or was she really here?

"I'm sure your family's okay," Pedar said, breaking into her thoughts. "Especially if Urho took your advice and got everyone into the gravel pit."

Guiltily, Lisa realized that she hadn't even been thinking about how her family was doing; she'd just assumed they were fine. They'd survived the fire before, but now that Pedar had brought it up, she wondered again if everything was the same. Admittedly, she was in totally unfamiliar territory here, but when it hit her what she'd been basing her lack of concern on, she almost laughed out loud: Michael J. Fox's experience in *Back to the Future*. The photo of Marty McFly and his brother and sister started to disappear when Marty had inadvertently changed history.

Unfortunately, she didn't have a Kodak compass to tell her if she was going in the right direction. She'd just assumed that she couldn't be here, couldn't have been born, if her grandma hadn't survived the fire.

Pedar was still looking at her, the concern evident on his ash-streaked face. Though red-rimmed and bloodshot from the smoke and wind, she was glad to see his left eye still held some of the twinkle that had caught her attention the first time she'd seen him. His right eye was ceremoniously covered with a gauze bandage, held by thick, white tape.

"I hope you're right. I hope they're okay," Lisa said. "What about your family? Where are they?" She remembered Pedar said he lived in a boarding house in Cloquet, but had never mentioned his parents or any brothers or sisters.

He didn't answer right away, and Lisa was afraid she'd said something wrong, again. Finally, he told her that both of his parents were dead, and his older brother, Emil, lived in Chicago with his wife, Anna.

"I'm going to have to send my sister-in-law a telegram when we get to Superior to let her know I'm all right. She'll be worried when she reads about the fire in the newspaper." Pedar went on to explain that his brother had been drafted in June. Emil had written Pedar, asking him to move to Chicago and stay with Anna while he was gone; he was sure Pedar could get a job at the stockyards, which was where Emil had been working before the draft.

"I may have to take him up on it, now. It doesn't look like I'll still have a job as a tote team driver this winter, let alone my job with the Companies Store. The whole west end of town was burning when we left, so I'm sure it's gone. Do you think the stockyards would hire a man with only one good eye?" Pedar asked with half a smile.

It had never occurred to Lisa that his eye injury might be permanent, or that Pedar might think it was. "Once we get to Superior, we'll get a doctor to look at your eye again. You're going to be fine," she said.

"Are you hungry?" Pedar asked, pulling something wrapped in a red handkerchief out of his jacket pocket. "I've got two of the sandwiches we made at the McClains' right here."

"Where did you get those? I thought Mary had all of the sandwiches."

"I took them when I held the bag for her when we went back in the house. You want one?"

Lisa hadn't had a thing to eat since she woke up in the field on her grandma's farm, and a ham sandwich would actually taste very good right now. But the thought of them sitting in Pedar's pocket all this time, no Baggie or Saran Wrap, and no refrigeration—she must have made a face, because Pedar started to laugh.

"What? It's a clean handkerchief," he said, unwrapping the two ham sandwiches, handing her one and taking a big bite out of the other. "Eat. You've got to be hungry. I know I am."

As Lisa watched him chew and swallow, then take another bite, her own hunger overcame her fear of botulism. She took a bite of the sandwich. The smoky, salty taste of the ham combined with the flaky, buttery taste of her great-grandma's biscuit was wonderful. It was possibly the best sandwich she'd ever eaten. Before she knew it, she was licking her fingers and the sandwich was gone.

"I guess I should have taken four," Pedar grinned.

She was sitting on his left, and he made an obvious effort to keep his bandaged right eye towards the window and away from her. He thought he had fooled her, and she allowed him to maintain his pride and think she hadn't seen through his sudden change of topics and offer of food. She knew both had much more to do with his concern about his eye and a lot less to do with his actually being hungry. If he didn't want to talk about it, fine. He must be in a lot of pain for him to be that worried, and Lisa promised herself she would do everything she could to help him once they got to Superior.

The ride from Carlton to Superior was slow and cautious, but much less eventful, less stressful than their ride in the boxcar from Cloquet to Carlton. The fire had turned towards the Woodland, Lakeside, and Lester Park areas of Duluth, the smoke blowing thick and heavy across the bay to Superior, much like the fog that usually rolled in off the lake.

The train finally pulled into the Superior depot at 3:30 the morning of October 13. It had been five hours since they'd left Cloquet, and Lisa felt dirty and exhausted. She craved a shower and a nice soft bed with crisp white sheets, thick warm blankets, and plump down pillows.

Wisconsin State Guards held back the crowds, allowing only Red Cross workers to meet the trainload of refugees with blankets and immediate medical assistance. The surgical masks they all wore on their faces were a frightening reminder that the fire wasn't the only threat facing them tonight. Lisa remembered what Pedar told her earlier, that on Friday both Duluth and Superior prohibited public gatherings to try and limit the Spanish flu epidemic.

The most seriously injured were taken immediately by ambulance to St. Mary's and St. Francis Hospitals, while those with less severe injuries were herded into cars driven by civilian volunteers and taken to the armory and other public halls to register. Families had been split up, some escaping on different trains, some by foot, some by car, depending on where they were when the fire hit. Most of the phone and telegraph lines were gone. Registering, so that everyone could eventually find each other, was paramount.

The skinny young man who drove Lisa and Pedar to the armory introduced himself as Carl Mueller and asked them if they needed a place to sleep. "My mother and I have a house not too far from here if you want to stay with us," he explained. "It's just down Belknap. We'll go to the armory first so you can register and see a doctor; then it's just a couple of blocks from there. Your sister can have my room and you can sleep on the sofa. I'll take the floor."

"Oh, we're not…"

"Thanks," Pedar interrupted, "we appreciate the offer. But you take the sofa and I'll sleep on the floor."

Why did Pedar want the Muellers to believe they were brother and sister? Lisa wasn't sure, but she decided to let it go for now—he must have his reasons.

While Carl and Pedar made casual conversation about everything but the fire, Lisa sat alone in the backseat, wondering what was going to happen now. She'd made it to Superior. She was fine; Pedar was fine. How and when were the two of them going to disappear? Could it be that Carl and his mother were really cannibal serial killers? Or maybe it was something as simple as getting hit by another car on this extraordinarily busy night.

Wow, she thought as they approached the armory, I'm either really tired, or all this smoke is making me delirious.

16
Chapter

A registration table had been set up in the front of the armory, which was crowded with cots, tired refugees, and Red Cross personnel.

"Just sign your names, and where you're staying, so your friends and relatives can find you," said the Red Cross woman behind the table, mumbling through her white surgical mask.

Carl gave them his address and telephone number, which both Pedar and Lisa diligently wrote down, and signed their names, Pedar's at the bottom of one page, and Lisa's at the top of a new page. Lisa never would have guessed that Pedar spelled his name P-e-d-a-r-O-l-e-s-o-n, and not P-e-t-e-r-O-l-s-o-n, if she hadn't seen his signature on the page that she moved to the bottom of the stack so she could sign her name, well actually, her great-aunt's name. She also saw that if the pages got separated, or put in a different order, no one would be able to tell she and Pedar had come here together.

"We're putting together a known-casualty list, on the wall over there," said the woman, pointing at sheets of paper taped to the wall on her right. "Not all of the names have been confirmed, but we're asking everyone to take a look at it. If you know someone who should be on it but isn't, we'll add their name. Every name on the list must have a signature so we can go back and verify the identification."

"Can we take a look at the people who've already registered?" Pedar asked the woman. To Lisa, he added, "I want to see if Mrs. McClain signed in here."

"Go ahead, that's what it's for." The woman turned to help the next refugee in line.

While Pedar scanned the registration sheets, Lisa looked around the room, hoping to at least see someone she recognized, anyone she'd seen before, on the train, at the depot, in Carlton, but there was no one. Carl patiently stood to the side, talking with a neighbor who was also waiting to bring someone home for the night.

"Liisa! Mrs. McClain, Michael, and Mary were here. They're staying with a family named Lawrence. Here, write down this number so we can call them and let them know we're okay."

The Red Cross woman behind the table handed her a piece of paper and a pencil, and Lisa obligingly wrote down the phone number Pedar read off to her.

"Is there a doctor who can see us?" Lisa asked, and the woman pointed at a line that stretched like a human snake along one side of the armory floor.

"It'll take too long," Pedar said shaking his head, "and you're tired. We can come back tomorrow. I'm sure they'll still be here."

"We're here now and you need to see a doctor. Let's get in line. I can sit on the floor if I get tired of standing." She'd stood in lines a lot longer than this to get on rides at Disney World. Where, she thought as she and Pedar took their place at the back of the line, was the FASTPASS when you needed one?

Carl went home to tell his mother he was bringing back two guests. The line moved slowly, and Lisa longed to stretch out and go to sleep. By the time it was finally their turn to see the doctor, she could barely keep her eyes open.

One doctor and three nurses had set up a temporary examination station in one corner of the armory. Pedar was lucky enough to see the doctor, who was on retainer with one of the railroads and familiar with removing cinders and other flying objects from eyes.

"It doesn't look like you actually injured the cornea, but I want to make sure," the doctor said, examining Pedar's eye with a magnifying glass. He reached in his black bag and pulled out a small brown glass bottle, put an eyedropper in the bottle, and filled it half way with the orange-red colored liquid from the bottle.

"What is that? Will it hurt? What's it supposed to do?" Lisa asked, her Aunt Shirley's voice playing like a tape in her head.

A nurse at the Raiter Clinic, Shirley always said, "If a doctor doesn't tell you what he or she's doing, you have to ask. Every patient has the right to know what a treatment can or is supposed to do."

The doctor frowned and looked more than a little annoyed that anyone, let alone a girl, was questioning what he was doing. "It's flourescin. If the cornea has been injured, the area will turn a greenish color. If there's no injury, it stays clear. Now if you don't mind."

"Is it going to hurt?" Lisa persisted. She could see that Pedar was becoming embarrassed, but she wanted to know.

"No, when I first flushed out the eye, I used a boric acid solution with a small amount of cocaine. He won't feel a thing."

"Cocaine?!" Lisa was incredulous.

"Standard procedure," he said, his defiant tone daring her to challenge him again, and began to put the drops into Pedar's eye.

"Just as I thought," he said moments later. "No real injury; just a small corneal abrasion. The cornea heals pretty fast. Keep it bandaged for at least the next twelve hours. You'll be fine in a day, two at the most."

17
Chapter

"Are you too tired to look at the casualty list now?" Pedar asked Lisa after they'd left the doctor. "Maybe we should come back tomorrow after more names have had a chance to be verified."

"Let's get it over with as long as we're here. We can come back tomorrow and look at it again, if you think we have to." Lisa knew she wouldn't know anyone on the list, so it really didn't matter to her.

She and Pedar walked over to the handwritten lists on the wall, but only Pedar read them. His hand shook as his finger stopped at a name he recognized. He kept reading, and his finger stopped again at another name. This time he turned and looked at Lisa, his face white with anguish.

"What? Who is it? It's not Ada and the baby, is it?" Lisa's eyes followed his finger, still pointing at the name on the wall: Mrs. William Maki and five children.

"There's got to be more than one William Maki family. It can't be my family," Lisa protested. It wasn't true; her family couldn't be dead. She knew she couldn't be here if her grandma had died in the fire; it was as simple as that.

"Eino Oja signed it. His farm is just down the road from your mother's," Pedar said gently, putting his hand on her arm. "Liisa, I'm so sorry."

"No, Pedar, the list is wrong. Mr. Oja's wrong." Lisa needed him to understand, but she could tell from his face that he accepted the list as fact, and dismissed her denials as shock. There wasn't a phone at their farm or at their neighbors, the Koskis'. And even if they had a phone, the phone lines were gone. She had no way to check on her family without physically travelling back to Cloquet, back to the farm. Lisa felt so helpless. She could only imagine how Liisa had felt.

"Carl's back. Come on. We both need some sleep. Later today, we'll try and get a hold of Mrs. McClain; she'll know what to do." Pedar put his arm around her waist and led her to the spot where Carl stood waving his arms near one of the armory doors.

The three of them drove to Carl's house in silence. Neither Pedar nor Lisa knew what to say, and Carl—sensing that *something* had happened—didn't ask.

Mrs. Mueller greeted them at the door wrapped from neck to toes in a burgundy and gray flannel bathrobe with a matching belt tied at her plump, round waist; her hair tidily tucked into a white linen cap that looked like a shower cap. She reminded Lisa of what Mrs. Claus would look like if she were real. "You two must be exhausted! Liisa, I've made up Carl's room for you, and Carl and Pedar will sleep in the living room. Carl thought you might be hungry, so I put out some bread and butter and heated up some vegetable soup."

Carl and Mrs. Mueller went to bed, leaving Lisa and Pedar alone at the kitchen table. The soup smelled wonderful, but Lisa didn't think she could eat a thing. Instead, she played with her spoon, stirring her soup around and around in the bowl, much like her stomach was twisting itself around and inside out. Her mind was racing, and even though she was exhausted, she knew she couldn't possibly sleep. If everything happened for a reason, what was she doing here? Was history repeating itself, or had she somehow caused it to take a detour, affecting the final outcome, affecting her life? Would she ever see her family—Lisa Hanson's family—again?

"So," she said, trying to think about something else, anything else, "why did you want Carl to think you were my brother?"

"Until I can get you back to Mrs. McClain, you're my responsibility. It's just not right, two people traveling together who aren't related. So I think it's best that the Muellers think we're family."

"I see." Lisa saw only too well. He cared about her (that was obvious), but not in the way she wanted him to. What seemed to concern him the most was what other people might think. And, even after all they'd been through together today, it still seemed to her that he felt like he was babysitting. He probably couldn't wait to get rid of the responsibility.

Lisa reached in the pocket of her skirt and pulled out the piece of paper that held the phone number she'd copied from the registration list at the armory.

"Let's call Mrs. McClain. Here's the number," she said handing it to him. "I hope the Mueller's won't mind if we use their phone."

"Now? Liisa, it's 6:00 in the morning."

"Do you really think anyone's sleeping after all that's happened?"

"No, probably not, but you need to get some sleep. I need to get some sleep. We can call her later."

"I'd really like to call her now and let her know we're okay. I'm sure she's worried about me, about us. Especially if she saw my family on the list at the armory."

Pedar took the piece of paper over to the phone and called the number where the McClains were staying.

"They were here," the voice at the other end of the phone told Pedar, "but they left around 5:00 this morning to stay with some friends in Duluth. Mrs. McClain left the phone number of where they went, but I don't know where I put it. Could you call back later? Or check with the Red Cross; maybe Mrs. McClain has re-registered."

"The Red Cross should know where they are," Pedar said after he hung up. "Mrs. McClain is probably working with them. I'll go check at the armory later this morning and see if I can get a hold of her. If I can't find her, what are you going to do? Do you have any family in the area you can stay with?"

Lisa shook her head. Liisa's father and mother had come to America alone and started their family here. And Lisa didn't know anyone but the McClains and Pedar.

"Are you going to Chicago to stay with your sister-in-law?" she asked.

"Yes, there's no reason for me to go back to Cloquet. My job is gone. Mrs. Tillman's boarding house is gone, and all the money I was saving with it. In fact, I'm going to have to ask my sister-in-law to wire me money for a train ticket."

The two of them sat back down at the kitchen table, neither of them saying anything for several minutes. Looking at that ridiculous gauze patch over his right eye and the despair on his face, she felt a lump begin to form in her throat.

Finally Lisa broke the silence. She needed to know why Liisa had never gone back to Cloquet, why she hadn't at least tried to bury her family. "I don't have any money either. How am I going to bury my family?" she asked, her voice catching.

"There's nothing you can do," Pedar said. "A sheet on the wall at the armory, next to the casualty list, said the Minnesota Home Guard is going to bury all of the dead, and because of the flu epidemic, there can't be any public funeral services."

Well, Lisa thought, that explains why Liisa never found out her family was still alive. She must have assumed the casualty list at the armory was correct. But where did she go? What did she do?

"Liisa?"

"I'm sorry Pedar, I was just…"

"Thinking about your family," he finished for her. "No, I'm sorry. I've been so busy trying to figure out what I should do—I just wasn't thinking about all you've lost. I'm really sorry about your family."

"Thanks," she said, then added, "and I'm sorry for being so much trouble. You were right, I should have gotten on the train with Mrs. McClain."

"Actually, it's probably good you came with me," Pedar said, surprising her for the second time since she'd met him. "I think Ada really appreciated having another woman along."

Another woman. He'd called her a woman! Okay, so he hadn't exactly said *he* was glad she'd come with him, but he had called her a woman. It was a start, and she'd settle for that for now. Maybe there was hope yet that he could, that he would, think of her in a more romantic way.

"After we get some sleep, we'll go looking for Mrs. McClain. If we can't find her," Pedar continued, "I guess I'll have to take you with me to Chicago. We'll leave Emil and Anna's address and phone number with the Muellers in case the McClains look for us. I don't know what else to do. Anna works for a dressmaker; I'm sure—if we have to—she can get you a job. And I should be able to get a job at the stockyards."

So that's what happened, Lisa thought, staring at her hands. It was all so clear now. Thinking her family was dead, and with no job or place to live, Liisa had gone with Pedar to Chicago. What a relief! All this time Liisa's family thought something terrible had happened to her, and she thought they'd died in the fire; neither of them true.

With all the answers she'd received tonight, Lisa didn't think she could sleep. She lay in bed, wearing an old flannel nightgown Mrs. Mueller had loaned her for the night, staring at the Maki family photo she'd put on the bedside table, thinking about her family, thinking about going to Chicago with Pedar. Was she doing the right thing? Was she doing what Liisa had done? She was so close to finding out what had happened, she felt if she stretched out her hand she could touch the final answer—the reason she was here.

She must have fallen asleep at some point, for the next thing she knew the sun was shining pink through her closed eyelids and someone was calling her name.

"Lisa. Wake up. You've been asleep for almost eighteen hours. I'm taking you up to the Raiter Clinic and have a doctor check you over and give you a prescription. Shirley was telling me about these new flu medications that are available. If you start taking them within the first forty-eight hours, they're supposed to lessen the severity and length of the flu by a couple days."

Lisa opened her eyes to see her mother standing over her. She was back in her bedroom. She'd been sleeping for eighteen hours? It must have been a dream after all.

"How are you feeling?" her mother asked.

"Like death warmed over," Lisa moaned, closing her eyes again. Her head was throbbing, and muscles and joints were aching where she'd never even known she had muscles or joints.

"Come on, Sarah Bernhardt, stop acting like a drama queen and get dressed."

"Can't you just ask Shirley to call in a prescription to the drug store and then you can go pick it up? Why do I have to go to see a doctor? I'd rather stay here in bed. I feel..."

"Like death warmed over," her mother finished for her. "I know, you told me. I really want a doctor to look you over. So get dressed and I'll go get the car."

Lisa wasn't sure she had enough energy to even get out of bed, let alone change her clothes. She lay in bed, willing herself to sit up; it wasn't working. A horn honked outside, and Lisa knew her mother was waiting for her in the car. She slung her legs over the side of the bed and stood wobbly, threw off her sweatpants, pulled on her jeans, and slid her feet into her sneakers. She felt lightheaded and decided seeing a doctor was probably a good idea after all.

The clinic waiting room had two other flu victims ahead of her, and Lisa sat with them waiting for her turn to see the doctor. Thirty minutes later she was in a small exam room, a thermometer in her mouth and her left sleeve rolled up, getting her blood pressure checked by a nurse in a crisp white pants uniform. Quite a difference from the makeshift hospital in Carlton, she thought, amazed by how real her dream seemed and that she could remember so much of it.

"The doctor will be in to see you in just a minute," the nurse said. She removed the thermometer from Lisa's mouth and jotted something down on a piece of paper attached to a clipboard, then left.

"Hey," her Aunt Shirley poked her head in the room. "How you doing kiddo?"

"I'll live, I think. But right now, I'm not sure I want to." Lisa offered a weak smile.

"Don't worry, Dr. Swanson will take care of you. He's new in town, but he knows his stuff. And here he comes now."

A tall auburn-haired man wearing a white lab coat and a stethoscope around his neck stepped into the doorway and smiled.

"Dr. Swanson," Shirley said, "this is my sister, Louise Hanson, and her daughter, Lisa. Lisa's got the flu."

"Hi. Peter Swanson," the doctor said shaking Mrs. Hanson's hand. Turning to Lisa, he said, "You're my eighth flu patient this week. The flu season's early this year and it's packing quite a wallop. Believe me, I know, my son was one of the first victims."

Peter Swanson. Why did that name sound so familiar? Lisa tried to think, but couldn't quite place it.

Dr. Swanson looked at the clipboard, then said, "It says here you started feeling sick after school yesterday afternoon. I'm going to get you started on Tamiflu. Take one capsule twice a day—once in the morning and once at night—for five days."

"What exactly does it do?" Lisa asked.

Dr. Swanson smiled at Lisa, then looked at her Aunt Shirley. "I see you've already got her trained."

He turned back to Lisa. "It shortens the time you'll have the flu by about a day and a half and reduces the severity of your symptoms by thirty to forty percent besides reducing complications. Some people experience nausea, vomiting, or diarrhea. But taking the capsule with food should help. My son Peter's been taking it and he hasn't had any problems. And, I think it's made a difference."

Ah, Peter Swanson…!

"I think your son's in my Spanish class," Lisa said.

"He does take Spanish. We just moved here from Denver, so if you have a new kid in your class, that's probably him."

"Tell them why you moved to Cloquet," Shirley said.

"I told your aunt that my grandparents used to live in Cloquet. They moved to Coeur d'Alene, Idaho, after the fire—followed the timber industry out West. About a year ago, my wife and I decided we needed to get out of the city—we both wanted to move to a small town, preferably in the Midwest. So when I heard about an opening in Cloquet, I applied. It was the small town we were looking for with the added bonus of my family's history here."

"Your own version of *Roots*, Scandinavian style," Shirley said laughing.

"I have an aunt, a sister, and a niece named Lisa," Dr. Swanson said to Lisa.

"Oh." Lisa wasn't sure what, if anything, she was supposed to say.

"There's been a Lisa and a Peter in my family ever since the fire."

If he didn't have it before, Dr. Swanson suddenly had Lisa's undivided attention.

"Really? Why?" her mother asked.

"Family history says a young couple named Peter and Lisa saved my grandparents' lives the night of the fire by driving them to the train in a car. My grandma was not only pregnant, she'd sprained her ankle and couldn't walk. She went into labor that night and delivered my father. They named him Peter, for obvious reasons. Their next child, a girl, they named Lisa. According to my grandpa, without the first Peter and Lisa, none of us Swansons would be here. And my grandma always said she would never have made it through that awful train ride out of town if Lisa hadn't been with her.

"The names Peter and Lisa have become more than a family tradition, it's almost a mandate. The first boy in the family is named Peter, and the first girl is named Lisa. My son, Peter, was the first boy grandchild. My brother Charles' daughter, Lisa, was the first girl grandchild."

"What happened to the original Peter and Lisa? Did your families stay in touch?" Lisa's mother asked.

"My grandpa said they both disappeared the night of the fire. No one knows what happened to them."

I do, thought Lisa. I know what happened to them, or at least what I think happened to them. Wow! Was it possible she'd really been there, in the past? Even more amazing, that Dr. Swanson could be her friend, Ada's, grandson?

"You know," Shirley said looking first at Lisa, then at Dr. Swanson, "you told me earlier that your son is interested in learning more about the fire. Lisa's kind of the family history buff, isn't she, Louise? Both of her dad's parents were kids at the time of the fire. Maybe she could fill your son in on what she knows about the fire, once she feels a little better, of course."

"Peter's kind of shy, and he misses his old friends in Denver. He hasn't made many new friends here yet. I'd really appreciate it if you'd be willing to share what you know about the fire with him." Dr. Swanson smiled at Lisa, whose face suddenly felt like it was on fire.

All three of them were looking at her, waiting for her to say something. If she said yes, there would be no way she could get out of it, and she couldn't quite remember what the Peter Swanson in her Spanish class looked like. In the back of her mind, she saw him as tall with his father's auburn-colored hair and, if she remembered correctly, actually pretty cute. And now that she thought about it, it was possible that she and her friends had mistaken his shyness for being stuck-up.

Lisa looked at Dr. Swanson and saw with amazement that he had bright green eyes with little brown flecks that glowed like gold, just like Ada. She wondered if his son, Peter, had the same eyes. They both had Ada's auburn-colored hair. "Okay," she said. "I'll talk to him when I get back to school."

Dr. Swanson scribbled his signature on a prescription pad, tore off the top sheet and handed it to Lisa's mother. "Thank you, Lisa. Peter really needs to start getting out and meeting people. I hope you two become friends."

When she finally got home and crawled back into bed, Lisa was exhausted. She reached down to the end of the bed where she had kicked her grandma's quilt, and saw it as if for the first time. The trapezoid-shaped piece of fabric in the center of the quilt, royal blue with tiny white flowers, was exactly like the scarf she had given her Grandma Inga to keep the hair out of her face. The plain caramel-colored fabric to the right looked just like the skirt Helen Maki had been wearing the day of the fire. And this piece was the color of Arvo's shirt; this one Urho's shirt. Here was her Grandma Inga's dress, and these pieces looked like the red and blue dresses Hannah and Ida had been wearing. All the clothes the Maki family had been wearing the day of the fire were here in the quilt.

Further out from the center, she saw material from Mrs. McClain's skirt, Mary's dress, Michael's shirt, and even Ada's green dress. Plus, she remembered her grandma used the blanket that had saved her in the gravel pit as the batting for the inside. Her grandma had sewn her memory quilt using actual memories from the day of the fire. Something from everyone Liisa touched that day was here. In hindsight now, with all she knew, with all she'd experienced, it seemed so right that her grandma had entrusted Lisa, her sister's namesake, with the care of these precious memories.

Everyone but Pedar was represented in that quilt. But if her suspicions were right, Liisa and Pedar ended up together. With all the chaos, and the phone and telegraph lines to Cloquet gone, they must never have been able to locate Mrs. McClain, so Liisa had gone with Pedar to stay with his sister-in-law in Chicago. Lisa had a feeling that Pedar had begun to see Liisa in a new light—a possibly more grown-up, more romantic light—and after all that happened the day before, Lisa was pretty confident she could trust her feelings.

Everything happened for a reason—both her grandma and Ada had told her that—and she knew now there were at least two reasons she'd seen the past. First, and most important of all, she thought she knew what happened to her grandma's oldest sister, and once she felt better, she was going on the Internet to see if her father could have cousins—that no one else knew existed—in Chicago with the last name Oleson. Bringing the family back together would have been important to her grandma, so it was important to Lisa.

Second, two connections to Ada in one day had to mean something. Meeting Dr. Swanson and finding the clothes Ada was wearing that day were part of her grandma's quilt—there was no such thing as a coincidence.

Maybe she was supposed to meet the younger Peter Swanson. Maybe they were supposed to be friends. Maybe—

If everything happened for a reason, she couldn't wait to see what was going to happen next. If nothing else, the next couple of weeks were going to be very interesting; very interesting indeed.

The End

Maki—Hanson Family Tree

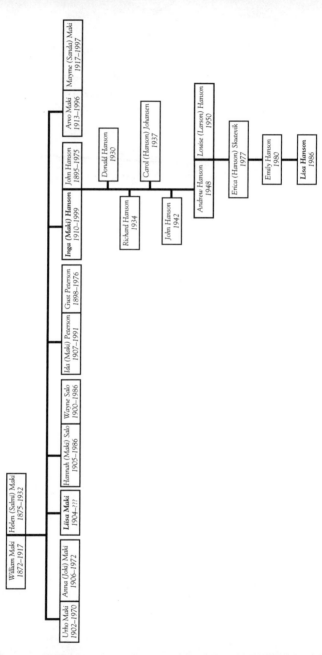

Resources

ARTICLES & JOURNALS

Benson, G.E. "Corneal Injuries." *Railway Surgical Journal*. 1916-1917, xxiii, pages 286-291.

Da Costa, J.C. "The effects of the inhalation of smoke and of irritating and poisonous gases by firemen, and the proper treatment of the results." *Therapeutic Gazette*. 1903, xix, pages 153-160.

Eelman, Anna. "Of Sackers & Sackcloth." *Quilt World*, September 1998; pp. 8-9, 14.

Eelman, Anna. "For the Love of Feedsacks." *Patchwork Quilts*, July 1995, pp. 43-44.

Elfes Gray, Kathryn. "Fifty Years of Progress Since 1918 Holocaust." *Cloquet Pine Knot*, October 10, 1968, pp. 1-2.

Hermance, G.E. "Fractures and sprains of the ankle and their treatment." *Railway Surgical Journal*. 1917, xxiii, pages 146-150.

Hemingson, Ray E. *Death by Fire*. Palmer Publications, Inc. 1983.

Hoover, Florence Anderson. "The Forest Fire of Oct. 12, 1918." *Cloquet Pine Knot*, October 10, 1968, pp. 4.

Niemi, Harriet. "Awfullest fire horror in state's history." Cloquet Public Library. 1977.

Reprinted from *The Potlatch Story*. "Sixty-six years ago Cloquet burns to the ground." *Pine Knot-Billboard*. October 11, 1984, pp. 1-2.

Sommer, Barbara. "The City That Really Came Back—Cloquet and the Fires of 1918." Carlton County Historical Society, History Week, February 1985.

Stapel, Jane Clark. "A Brief History of the 'Feedsack.'" www.planetpatchwork.com/feedsack.htm

Star-Gazzette. "Cloquet—Home of the White Pine, Queen City of the St. Louis." Originally published in 1907. Special Limited Edition reprinted 1979.

Stewart-Taylor Co. "Lights and shadows in the history of Cloquet; the city that really came back; a romance of the Minnesota Arrowhead country." 1923.

BOOKS

Carroll, Francis M. *Crossroads in Time. A History of Carlton County, Minnesota.* Chapter 10: "The Great 1918 Fires." Cloquet, MN: The Carlton County Historical Society. 1987.

Carroll, Francis M. and Raiter, Franklin R. *The Fires of Autumn. The Cloquet-Moose Lake Disaster of 1918.* Minnesota Historical Society Press. 1990.

Cook, Anna Lue. *Identification and Value Guide to Textile Bags (The Feeding and Clothing of America).* Books Americana. 1990.

Holbrook, Stewart Hall. *Burning an empire, the story of American forest fires.* The Macmillan Company, 1943. Chapter Three: The Story of Cloquet, pages 31-45. Chapter Four: Smoke in the Clearing, pages 46-53.

Houck, Carter. *The Quilt Encyclopedia.* H.N. Abrams in association with the Museum of American Folk Art. 1991.

Lambert, Carol Illikainen. *Firebeast: The Fires of 1918*. Moose Lake Area Historical Society. 1994.

Olin, JoAnne. Editor. *Everyday Fashions 1909-1920. As Pictured in Sears Catalog*. Dover Publications, Inc. 1995.

O'Meara, Walter. *We made it through the winter: a memoir of northern Minnesota boyhood*. Minnesota Historical Society. 1974.

COLLECTIONS

Photo Collection, Minnesota Historical Society

Quilt Collection, Minnesota Historical Society

INTERNET SITES

The American Experience_Influenza_1918:
www.pbs.org/wgbh/pages/amex/influenza

Flu deaths rivaled, ran along side World War I (3/10/1997):
www.sciencenews.org/sn_arc97/3_22_97/fob1.htm

The History of the Telephone:
http://hyperarchive.lcs.mit.edu/telecomarchives/tribute/the_history_of_the_telephone.html

The Influenza Pandemic of 1918:
http://www.stanford.edu/group/virus/uda/

Life at Camp Funston: http://www2.okstate.edu/ww1hist/

Tamiflu: www.tamiflu.com

MEMOIRS & PERSONAL INTERVIEWS

Cloquet Fire Sufferers. "A Group of Essays." The Women's Friday Club, Cloquet, Minnesota. 1935.

Erickson, Ingrid (Jokela). 1909–1994. Personal interview with fire survivor.

Evenson, Louise (Franklin). 1914–. Personal interview with fire survivor.

Gellerman, Beatrice Parks. "Memoirs of Beatrice Parks Gellerman." Austin, MN: People's Publishing. 1996.

Gray, Kathryn Elfes. "Family facts and fancies: also legends, lore, and lies." 1959. Reminiscences, newspaper columns and excerpts, and miscellaneous writings of Kathryn Elfes Gray (who also wrote under an earlier name, Kathryn Elfes Casher) relating primarily to the forest fire which destroyed Cloquet, Minnesota, in 1918. Minnesota Historical Society Collection.

Harney, Rosella. "Rosella Harney relates fire experience." *Pine Knot-Billboard*. October 11, 1984, pp. 3, 10.

Lavasseur, Sister Marie. "Sister remembers the fire." *Pine Knot-Billboard*. October 11, 1984, pp. 3, 10.

Panger, Sister Alicia. "I remember the great fire; our lives were not among the 608 lost." *The Catholic Digest*. January 1964.

NEWSPAPERS

Cloquet Pine Knot. January–December, 1918.

Duluth Herald. January–December 1918.

Duluth News Tribune. January–December 1918.

Superior Telegram. October 13–14, 1918.

VIDEOS

The Fires of 1918 Revisited—Oral Histories by Cloquet Area Survivors, hosted by Harriet Niemi. Cloquet Public Library and Carlton County Historical Society. 1993.

The Fires of 1918 Revisited—Oral Histories, hosted by Barbara Sommer. Interviews with Paul Wagtskold and Jennie Kolseth Wagtskold. Carlton County Historical Society. n.d.

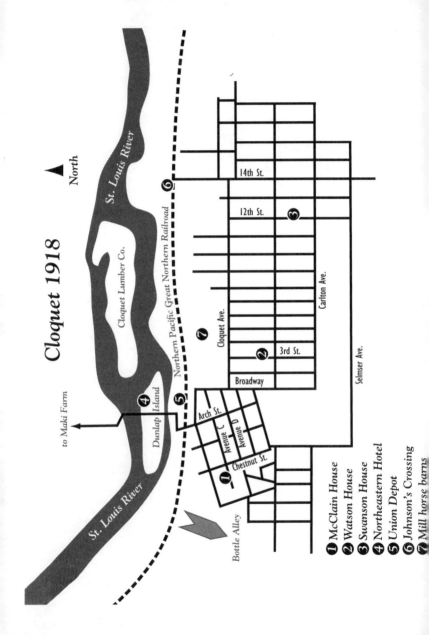

Cloquet 1918

North

St. Louis River

Cloquet Lumber Co.

St. Louis River

to Maki Farm

Dunlap Island

Northern Pacific Great Northern Railroad

Bottle Alley

Arch St.

Avenue C

Avenue D

Chestnut St.

Broadway

3rd St.

Cloquet Ave.

Carlton Ave.

Selmser Ave.

12th St.

14th St.

❶ McClain House
❷ Watson House
❸ Swanson House
❹ Northeastern Hotel
❺ Union Depot
❻ Johnson's Crossing
❼ Mill horse barns